'What's that?'

Clare held out the frame in silence. There was no explanation she could give that would not involve awkwardness. He took it from her and she said, 'I'm sorry . . .' her voice shaky with emotion. Every fibre of her being was aware of his reaction. She saw the tiny movement of the muscle of his jaw clench as he looked down at the face of his wife. She felt that she could sense his breathing change, his heartbeat alter. The temperature in the room fell in an instant, she was sure. 'It was in one of the drawers . . .' Her voice faltered into silence.

'And you were curious.' His eyes were cold and without feeling as he looked at her. 'You will have to remain so. Your concern is with the present, not the past.'

Another book you will enjoy
by ALISON YORK

THE MAXTON BEQUEST

For the first time in her life, Ros really felt as though she had a home. And then Dax Maxton appeared, with his good looks and his charm and his easy assumption that money could buy anything he wanted. And he wanted to turn Ros's life upside-down!

SUMMER IN EDEN

BY

ALISON YORK

MILLS & BOON LIMITED
ETON HOUSE 18-24 PARADISE ROAD
RICHMOND SURREY TW9 1SR

All the characters in this book have no existence outside the imagination of the Author, and have no relation whatsoever to anyone bearing the same name or names. They are not even distantly inspired by any individual known or unknown to the Author, and all the incidents are pure invention.

First published in Great Britain 1990
by Mills & Boon Limited

This edition 1990

ISBN 0 263 76595 4

Set in Times 11 on 12 pt.
01 – 9003 – 58450

Typeset in Great Britain by JCL Graphics, Bristol

Made and Printed in Great Britain

CHAPTER ONE

CLARE'S hands hovered over the keys of the typewriter as she paused to listen to the raised voice coming from Adam Melvin's office. Her day's temping at Breckland Associates had certainly not been without incident! Understandably put out by his normal secretary's bad timing—she had gone down with 'flu the day before he was due to go off on holiday himself—he had kept his frustration on a tight rein all day, but now the control seemed to have snapped and he was positively shouting down the phone.

'What the hell am I supposed to do about it at this late hour?' she heard, as clearly as though he were in the room with her. 'Everywhere closed, and all the arrangements made for tomorrow . . .' There was a pause, then, 'Don't expect any sympathy from me, you fool. I hope it hurts like hell!' The phone clattered down.

Clare pulled a face of pained sympathy for whoever was on the receiving end, then went back to her work and rattled off the final words of the script she had been typing. You could say this for Breckland Associates, she thought as she rolled the finished pages out of the machine, typing scripts was a whole lot more interesting than the average business letter. The company seemed to make documentaries on controversial issues, as far as she could gather. She grinned to herself. She had just had direct experience of how very controversial Mr

Melvin could be!

Perhaps the fact that she had done the impossible and completed the pile of work he had fed through to her all day would smooth him down a bit. It was to be hoped so, or whoever was waiting for him at home could be in for a bad time this evening.

He wasn't at first aware of her when she gave a gentle tap and stepped through into the adjoining office. He was staring at the Victorian print on the wall opposite his desk, not really seeing it, Clare could tell. A tall man, he had slumped down in his leather swivel chair, long legs thrust under the desk and in danger of tripping her up on the other side. His rather wicked, angular eyebrows were one of the first things she had noticed about him, and now they were drawn together, presumably as a direct result of the phone call she had overheard.

Clare bypassed the gleaming Russell and Bromley brogues, and it was only then that he stirred and registered her presence.

'Oh—still here, are you?' The quick smile—part of the charm that had kept her working cheerfully at twice her normal pace all day between crises—flashed out as he straightened up in his chair. 'Most of them shoot off like bats out of hell on Friday.'

'I've only just finished, Mr Melvin. These are the letters for signing—' Clare put the pile of immaculate correspondence in front of him and stood silently watching while he ran through them and slashed a bold, character-betraying signature at the foot of each page '—and this is the finished script.'

He flicked through the pages, eagle-eyed for any errors, and, finding none, murmured approval.

'At least something's gone right. I hadn't much hope of this lot being done today. Thank you—er—' He had forgotten her name.

'Clare—Clare Vincent,' Clare prompted, with the smile that transformed her rather grave, wide-eyed face and made people look twice in her direction. She really felt quite sorry for him. He had been bombarded with last-minute crises all day, and whoever had made the most recent call had obviously proved to be the last straw. 'Is there anything else I can do before I leave?' she added rashly.

He threw the script down with a slap on the desk and gave a half-rueful, half-exasperated laugh. 'Not unless you number driving on the right amongst your undoubted skills. Lord, what a mess!' He ran his hands through his hair, spiking it into glossy black tufts which Clare had an irrational urge to smooth down, then withdrawing again into his gloomy thoughts.

She felt the need to cheer him up and went on talking.

'I can boast an Advanced Driving Certificate—' she was rather proud of it '—but I haven't had the chance to try it out on the Continent yet.'

Suddenly he was seeing her again. 'Advanced? That's a weird thing for someone like you to have.'

Clare shrugged. 'I had the time, and the class was there. It was something to do.'

Adam Melvin was staring at her in a way that seemed oddly predatory. She felt uncomfortable.

'I suppose you're fixed up somewhere else for Monday?'

His eyes were a very dark blue . . . the colour of the sky at dusk, she realised.

'Not yet. I'm hoping there'll be something for me

when I go in to the agency.'

'You are?' His fingers drummed an absent-minded, uneven rhythm on the desk-top. 'So at the moment you're free . . .'

The door burst open and one of his colleagues walked in, saying, 'Are we going home this weekend or aren't we, then?' He saw Clare and grinned an apology at her. 'Sorry—I didn't realise there was anyone here. I just called in to say your lift's ready when you are, Adam, but you'd better run through this contract before you disappear into the back of beyond next week.'

Clare was hovering on the point of withdrawal, but Adam Melvin stopped her.

'Hang on a minute, Clare.' He turned back to his colleague. 'Scrap the lift for tonight, John, thanks all the same. I'm not through here—and there's something else I have to do. I'll get a taxi.'

'If you're sure. Enjoy your break, then.' He nodded a pleasant goodnight to Clare as he passed, and as soon as he was out of the room Adam Melvin got up and came over to her.

'I've a proposition to put to you.' She felt the force of his personality as he stood close, looking down at her, his dark blue eyes holding hers. 'I'd like to run through this contract first, though, so that I can shake the dust of this place off my feet. Can you bear to wait half an hour or so? Not here—along the road in the garden of the Drum and Monkey. It's beside the river, and I imagine the sun would be welcome after a day like this one. Will you do that?'

Clare blinked, resisting an odd impulse to step back away from him. 'Yes . . . I suppose so. If you like.'

He touched her shoulder lightly and smiled again.

'Good girl! No longer than half an hour—that's a promise.'

He had picked up the contract and was immersed in it before she closed the door.

A proposition . . . That was certainly a surprise, but then the past two days had been full of surprises, hadn't they?

For the first time since she had crossed the threshold of Breckland Associates, Clare allowed her mind to dwell on her own circumstances.

She had certainly surprised herself by walking out of the family home at Walberswick on the coast yesterday, and she must undoubtedly have surprised her father and Giles. She pictured them, dumbstruck, trying to imagine what madness could have made her desert the family home and her prospective husband as she had done. But of course, they wouldn't have let it throw the slightest of spanners in the works at the small publishing business they ran jointly. Business came before anything for both of them. Before people, before illness, before feelings . . . the lot. So let them wonder. For the moment she was keeping a low profile, as they said.

Clare collected her things and went along to the staff cloakroom to tidy up. Linda from the next office, who had sat with her at lunch and furnished an amazing amount of scandal centred on the Breckland employees, smiled at her through the mirror.

'Not sorry it's only been for one day, I expect?' she queried. 'I've heard a few of the fireworks through the wall. Our Mr Melvin doesn't seem to have been the easiest of people to handle today. He's had the devil in him for months, on and off, actually—not that I'm averse to a touch of that in a man. Losing his driving licence seems to have hit him slap-bang in the middle of his substantial ego. But that's men all over, isn't it? Take away their sex symbol of a car and they're practically castrated!'

Clare laughed as she ran a comb quickly through her heavy light brown hair, restoring it to its smooth, shining fall as her grey eyes met Linda's.

'How did he lose it? The driving licence, not the libido.'

'No idea. Probably behaving as though the road network was his and his alone. Don't they all? To be fair, it was around the time his wife died . . . so everything went wrong at once, I suppose. Don't take my prattling too seriously.' Linda snapped her bag shut. 'There, that's me sorted out ready to hit the road. Good luck with your new job.'

Left alone in the cloakroom, Clare looked at herself in the mirror, feeling a little lost. She was actually wearing her cream 'going away' suit—only the 'going away' for which it had been intended had taken an entirely different form.

Strange . . . Up to a certain point in her life, five weeks ago, she had always known what she was going to do in the future. Even when she had turned down her hard-worked-for university place, she had known exactly why, and what she was going to do instead. It was an empty feeling now to have a future that was a huge question mark, full of things she knew she didn't want to do rather than firm, positive ideas of the shape her life was to take.

When she had left Walberswick yesterday she had done what seemed the obvious thing at the time and got a single ticket to London. She could easily lose herself there for a while, she thought, and until she found a suitable place of her own to live she could stay in her father's company flat, for which she had a key. A day or two there would give her thinking time . . . stop her rushing into anything dreadful. Once on the train, though, she had realised that the company flat in St Katherine's Dock was the first place her father and Giles would think of looking for her. So she had got off at Ipswich, wasting the rest of her single to London, and had booked herself in at an unfortunate little guest-house for the night.

The following morning—this morning, though it seemed an age ago—she had gone to register at a temping agency, and it was pure chance that Adam Melvin had phoned in his urgent request for a replacement secretary at the speed of light just at the point when Clare had handed over her perfect skills test to the woman in charge. She had been sent haring over to Breckland Associates without the chance to draw breath.

At least hanging around to talk to him now would fill in a little time—and time certainly didn't stretch invitingly ahead at the moment. Apart from going through the local papers, she couldn't do anything more on the job front until the agency opened on Monday morning, and two days in a bed and breakfast place with her own confused thoughts was something she didn't relish in prospect.

It was a typical Suffolk day, the sky high, clear, and the palest of bluey-greys with only the lightest scattering of clouds over in the east, and the walk along to the pub was good after the high pressure of the day.

The Drum and Monkey was a half-timbered building with long gardens stretching down to the Gipping. There was a buzz of happy Friday chatter in the bar. Clare got herself a St Clement's, and took it down to a table on the riverbank where she could enjoy the sun.

She didn't have to wait long. Adam Melvin came striding round the corner of the pub, and a group of people leaving the gardens parted automatically to allow him through without pause.

I don't suppose it would occur to him to give way—in anything, Clare thought with amusement as she watched him approach. There was something slightly Mephistophelean about his whole face, she decided. The way his eyebrows rose to a sharply defined outer point . . . the slightly saturnine lines between nose and mouth . . . and the strong cleft in the chin combined to create the effect.

'What can I get you?' he called, detaining the barman with one hand.

'I'm fine, thanks.' She raised her glass, still three-quarters full, to show him.

With a quick, 'Just a pint of the local brew, then,' to the barman who had resumed his collecting of glasses, Adam joined her at the table, jumping straight to the point in a way the day had shown her was typical of him.

'You said you had no work fixed at the moment?'

'Nothing as yet. I'd only just enrolled at the agency when they had your call.'

He nodded. 'Providential for me. Any commitments?'

Clare looked warily at him over the rim of her glass. 'Such as?'

'Husband, family, attachments of any kind?'

'I'm pretty independent at the moment,' she said cautiously.

'So you could do anything you felt like doing without it depending on anyone else's say-so?'

'That would depend on a lot of things—not least

on whether I wanted to do whatever it is.'

He smiled, and again Clare registered the change that his smile effected. Not that he switched suddenly from devil to angel—there was still some hint of danger about him—but when his face relaxed like this she got a kind of red to amber feeling: proceed, but with caution.

'Cautious lady!' he said, the echo of her thoughts making her freeze for a moment until she remembered what she had said before her mind wandered. 'No . . . I haven't told you much as yet, have I?' he went on. 'I'll rectify that in a moment.'

There was a pause while the barman put a tankard of dark, frothy ale in front of him and Adam Melvin took a deep, grateful drink.

'That's good. Now, you told me about these driving qualifications of yours. How would you feel about driving abroad if you haven't done it before?'

Clare considered. 'I imagine I'd adjust without too much of a problem.'

'No tendency to do the sort of wild things the usual lady driver does?'

She raised her eyebrows at him. 'I think "the usual lady driver" is a pretty competent person. Not many of us end up——' she had been on the point of saying 'disqualified' when prudence curbed her tongue and she concluded '—being a danger to other road users. You can't say that about men with as much certainty.'

'I imagine we're both biased on that score. However, let me put my proposition to you. I need a driver for the next two weeks. I've made arrangements to complete some work we started on a foreign travel film of sorts—"we" being Breckland Associates, of course. The whole thing was scheduled to fit into my fortnight's time off, only the fool I'd engaged to ferry me around has gone and taken a tumble at squash and wrecked his wrist. Left it until the end of this afternoon when they'd finished putting him together at the Accident Unit to tell me, as well, the jackass. I'm absolutely stymied. With this damned suspension of mine I need a driver desperately, but how can I find someone between now and the flight I've got booked for tomorrow? The whole thing seemed to be crumbling round my ears—then up you pop with your throw-away remark about an Advanced Driving Certificate. You understand now, maybe, why your chance remark was so incredibly opportune?'

Clare understood all right, but she was rather taken aback by the thought of going off with this man, who had not exactly been the most relaxing of people to spend a day with, let alone two whole weeks. But the idea, she was quick to see, had advantages in her present circumstances. She played for time.

'If it's work, couldn't someone from Breckland go with you—someone you're used to working with?'

'In normal circumstances, yes. But this assignment is slightly delicate. As a matter of fact, the sponsors withdrew my team from the project before the work was completed to my satisfaction. In my opinion, the film isn't as good as it could be, but they say it will "do".' Adam frowned his disapproval of the attitude. 'Things don't "do" for me. They either succeed or they're scrapped.' The firm jaw was set, and Clare thought it would be difficult to come out on top in an argument with this man. 'I'd got this holiday fixed—arranged it while we were on the shoot because the place fascinated me so much. I can handle the filming myself, so I don't need any working associate as such—and I prefer not to involve anyone at Breckland because John—you saw him just now, and he's the other person involved at management level—is a much more cautious and amenable bloke than I am. He would say I was heading for trouble by not toeing the sponsors' line. Well, damn that for an idea. As far as I'm concerned, the film as it stands is trouble—and if there's one thing I'm determined about, it's that I won't have it going out as it is now with Breckland's credits on it. I intend to get it right, with no one any the wiser until it's too late for them to start interfering.'

Professional integrity, or plain vanity? Clare asked herself. Her question to him was much more discreet.

'Where is the filming to be done?'

'Ever been to Italy?'

Her eyes lit up. 'No, but I've always—intended to go some time. It sounds a wonderful country,' she concluded circumspectly.

'Never mind "some time". What about tomorrow? I'd pay you well and send in the sort of report on today to the agency that will ensure you more than enough work when you get back. And it won't exactly be a hardship to spend a couple of weeks in the sun.'

She looked thoughtfully at him. 'How would you take to being driven around by a woman? The driving I'm sure I could cope with, but hassle on the way I do it I could not stand.'

He gave a brief laugh. 'My dear Clare, you could be a one-eyed transsexual for all I care. What you would be to me is an animated driving licence, that's all. Don't let's get snarled up in trivialities. Is it yes or no? Time's short, I can't hang around all evening while you vacillate.'

Clare stood her ground. 'Be fair! I scarcely know you—we met today for the first time. I can't say the day's been without its ups and downs—and now you suggest that I go off into the middle distance with you. Might I also add that you phrase it all so charmingly! Is it to be wondered that I need to think about it?' The 'one-eyed transsexual' had stung rather.

'It's a job.' The devil look was beginning to etch itself on his face again. 'People take jobs all the time on the strength of one interview. Glad to get them too, most of them, these days. Come on—two weeks in the sun with nothing much to do but enjoy yourself for most of the time . . . Will you or won't you?' He was willing her to say yes, she could feel it, and she could also feel herself melting into acquiescence. But she had been down that road before, hadn't she?

'Give me five minutes to think. I need to get some change for the phone. I'll be back in a minute.' Clare jumped up and left him before he could stop her, going quickly indoors. She had plenty of change, but the only place she could think in peace without being badgered was the powder-room—not that she would really put it past this determined man to follow her there, come to think of it.

There was no one else in the cloakroom. She could argue with her reflection unobserved.

You've just got away from one impossible situation with a man, she told herself, and now you're more than half-way to walking into another one.

But this one was strictly limited. Two weeks. All right, two weeks in pretty forceful company, maybe, but two weeks out of the country and well away from her father and Giles. There was a lot to be said for it. And it was too much to expect that such an opportune offer should be perfect in every respect.

Yes, she could manage two weeks with Adam Melvin, just about, she decided. Her cases were still packed, back at the bed and breakfast place. Nothing could be easier, really. Not if you stifled all niggling doubts as to your own sanity, squashed the memory of the angry shouting down the phone, and resigned yourself to a bit of chauvinist resentment from the passenger seat.

And she had nothing to fear from him in the obvious way. Among the volume of scandal she had come out with at lunchtime, Linda had said that Adam Melvin had had no time for women since his wife's death. Was he bitter about what had happened, or a once-in-a-lifetime man? Clare wondered. She was inclined to think the latter. He must have loved a woman once or he would never have married at all, and such a tragically early end to the marriage, apart from being devastatingly sad, would make a man like him kick and shout against the fate that had dealt him such a blow. She would have to make allowances for him.

Someone came into the cloakroom and Clare quickly snapped out of her reverie. She outlined her mouth in pale coral and flicked a comb through her hair again. She had made her decision. Now she must make it known to Adam.

'Well?' The keen dark blue eyes raked her face when she sat down again at the table in the sun.

'All right, I'll take the job.'

'Just as well. I've been sitting here not coming up with a single alternative.' She was rather taken aback by the lack of gratitude. He seemd to have assumed that he would get what he wanted. He was now matter-of-factly ready to go on with the planning. 'What do you have to do?'

'Do?' she queried.

'Tell people. Pack your things. Any of the hundred and one things you women do when you go anywhere.'

'My things are still packed,' she told him coolly. 'And I have all the papers I'm likely to need here in this bag.' She patted her shoulder bag. 'So I shan't hold up proceedings tomorrow.'

He raised his devil's eyebrows. 'Looks as though you were counting on going somewhere.'

'No harm in being prepared,' she said briefly. She had no intention of being drawn on the subject of her own situation, and in any case it was far too long and involved a story to start telling a stranger.

'So where are all these ready-packed suitcases?'

'Quite local. I spent last night in a bed and breakfast place. Actually——' Clare's lovely warm smile broke out again '—I shall be very thankful not to have to spend more than one more night there. Mothballs, noisy plumbing and stale cornflakes don't add up to ideal conditions.'

'I'll call a cab and we'll collect your things. There's no need for any more nights at all in this dump you had the bad luck to stumble across. You'll come home with me tonight, of course.'

A wary shadow flickered across Clare's eyes. 'I don't think that's necessary. I'll be ready whenever you say, and I'll be perfectly all right there, honestly. I was exaggerating—it isn't as bad as all that.'

'Don't worry—it isn't your comfort, it's my own convenience I'm thinking about,' he said with wry bluntness. 'I'll even provide a chaperon, if that's what's worrying you—in the shape of my housekeeper, Mrs Kaye.' He looked quizzically at her. 'I can't promise to do that everywhere we go, though. Hang on here and I'll call a cab.'

He was off immediately, threading his way through the scattered tables, his broad shoulders and rapid stride challenging the world to thwart him if it dared.

Well, you've done it now, Clare told herself. He's not going to give you the slightest chance to change your mind. That's his real purpose in hanging on to you. Suddenly she felt extremely tired, not from the day itself, but from all that had led up to it. It had taken such an effort to tear herself away from her father and Giles, two men who were convinced they knew what was best for her. She had done that, at no small cost to her conscience in the circumstances, and now she seemed to have fallen into the grasp of another man in the same mould—a man who was single-minded in pursuit of his aims, and who seemed to have no hesitation in dragging others along in his wake.

But it's only for two weeks, she repeated to herself. I can stand anything for two weeks. The words lacked conviction.

He was back again, beckoning her from the corner of the pub.

'He'll be here in a couple of minutes. We may as well wait round the front. Damn all taxis and the need for them,' he added irritably. There seemed nothing safe to say on that subject.

'Where do you live?' asked Clare after a moment's

silence.

'In Lavenham—or a little way out of it. The house is called Monk's Eden. Here's the cab—come on.'

He took her arm and in the guise of helping her almost thrust her into the back of the cab, telling the driver where to go hot on the heels of the question he fired at her about the address of her bed and breakfast place.

No one, Clare thought with a ripple of amusement, could go along with Linda on the subject of cars and manhood—not where this particular man was concerned. Being deprived of his car certainly annoyed him, but it left him utterly, utterly male. She felt his displeasure as he settled in the back beside her, acting the part of unwilling passenger and drumming his fingers on the long, taut line of his thigh.

He looked at her suddenly. 'What's the joke?'

She jumped, foundering for a harmless explanation of her secret smile. 'The name of your house. I was thinking how strange it was. Monk's Eden . . .'

'The place is very old—had the name for centuries. I can claim neither credit nor blame.'

No, it wouldn't be your choice, Clare thought. Far too gentle and fanciful for you. She passed the time while the taxi crawled through the rush-hour traffic conjuring up a name to suit the man. Nothing monk-like, in spite of his non-involvement with the female of the species, and certainly nothing reminiscent of the innocence of the Garden of Eden, she thought.

She was very conscious of him at her side, even if she looked the other way out of the window. It was as though there was a field of energy surrounding him, alerting her own body to his presence.

Lucifer's Lair, she thought suddenly, stifling the urge to smile again. Yes, Lucifer's Lair, that was more like it. Suited him down to the ground.

She was about to shut her eyes to exclude the sight of his restless, impatient fingers when he turned and spoke to her.

'You won't regret coming with me, you know.'

'Of course not,' she said.

But she wondered. However, it was no good wondering now. It was happening, and that was that.

CHAPTER TWO

LAVENHAM was settling into its evening calm as they drove through the irregular streets, half-timbered houses with their clay and wattle filling glowing with the warmth of the late afternoon sun. Now that the shoppers had gone, the geese had reclaimed the patch in front of the baker's that traditionally belonged to them, and the sound of the bell-ringers' changes rang out from the high-steepled church.

About a mile beyond the town, Monk's Eden grew out of the landscape, mellow old bricks and twisted chimneys reflected in the moat that surrounded it so that house and water and curtain of trees blended together in a rippling, sparkling whole.

The cab crossed over the moat and stopped under an archway leading to a lawned courtyard, open on the far side so that Clare could see the curve of a bridge and beyond it velvet lawns and the graceful sweep of the fronds of willow trees, stirring in the light breeze. Beyond the willows soared the constrasting burnished brown of a copper beech and, to its right, the lavish pink candle-flowers of a horse-chestnut.

Eden indeed, Clare thought. Adam Melvin was dealing with the taxi fare while she absorbed the atmosphere of a place that seemed to reach out and draw her into its beauty.

'You must spend a lot of time on these lovely grounds,' she said as Adam joined her, walking over from the huddle of cases the cab-driver had left at the side of the cobbled archway.

'To the detriment of the house. I only use one wing of it. There were great plans for restoring the whole place once. Some day I'll get round to it. Come inside.'

He picked up the cases and led the way through a cool, almond-green carpeted hall and into the kitchen, dropping Clare's cases at the foot of the carved staircase.

Mrs Kaye seemed to be the kind of comfortable person who took most things in her stride, and a surprise visitor created no problems.

'The bed in the blue room is made up and aired. I'll just do a few more vegetables, then there's ample for two. No trouble at all,' she said, smiling warmly in acknowledgement of Clare's diffident apology for turning up unexpectedly. 'Poor Mr Forrester . . . he must be disappointed to be missing the trip,' she added, looking enquiringly at Adam.

'Poor nothing! I shan't lose any sleep over that,' Adam grunted. 'He's left me with a load of complications to sort out. We'd better see to those reservations straight away, Clare. Come through to the study and let's get it over with, will you?'

Mrs Kaye put a conspiratorial hand on Clare's arm as she obediently started after Adam. 'Take no notice of his bark. He'll be sending a crate of champagne round to that poor man if I know anything. When he's finished with you, give me the word and I'll take you upstairs.'

'Clare!' a voice called peremptorily from beyond the hall.

'Whoops!' Clare grinned at Mrs Kaye and ran dutifully off to track down where it came from.

The transfer of bookings didn't seem to offer any

problems, and once he had sorted that out Adam Melvin suggested that Clare should entertain herself once she had been shown her room. There were drinks in the sitting-room, she was told. Dinner would be at eight, and he had more than enough to keep him busy until then. Before she was out of the study, his head was bent over a jumble of papers on his desk and he appeared to be writing, reading and starting to dial a number on the phone simultaneously.

'How lucky you were free to go with Mr Melvin,' Mrs Kaye said as she led Clare upstairs. 'You'll be good company for him.' She gave a mischievous smile. 'He forgets how nice it can be to have a young lady around. All work, his life seems to be at present.'

She opened the door into a charming, low-ceilinged room at the end of the wing. 'Here we are. The wardrobe's empty, of course, and the bathroom next door is all yours. Mr Melvin has his own, so you won't be disturbed. Towels are in there, and there's a range of toiletries if you've forgotten anything. These drawers are empty, not that you'll be here long enough to need them, I suppose—oh, my goodness!' She had slid open the top two drawers of a chest near the window as she was talking, and now she was staring down into the second, disconcerted for the first time. She looked up at Clare. 'It's all right . . . I'd just forgotten all about this . . .' Slowly she picked up a photograph in a silver frame. 'It's—it was Mrs Melvin,' she corrected herself, obviously much moved by the sight of the photograph.

Clare stepped closer so that she could see the girl in the photograph, standing with a model's deceptively natural grace, at a three-quarter angle to camera, hands in the pockets of her loose, toffee-coloured trouser suit so that the jacket draped in silken folds revealing the ruffle-necked patterned blouse. Her cloud of tawny hair was blown back from her face, and there was a teasing, affectionate look in the dark-lashed hazel eyes, a smile on her mouth reminiscent of some past pleasure.

He took the photograph, Clare thought with absolute certainty. She was looking at him like that, both of them remembering whatever had prompted that smile.

A wave of sadness washed through her. Sadness for the kind of relationship captured in the picture, something she had never had. Sadness for the ending of it.

'She was lovely,' she said softly.

'Fay, she was called. It suited her. She wasn't much more than a girl—very warm . . . impulsive. She called me Katie.' Mrs Kaye put the photograph in the third drawer between lavender-scented pillowcases. 'I'll leave it here—I don't want to walk round the house with it when Mr Melvin's at home. He put away all her pictures . . . couldn't bear to look at them, I suppose. But this one was away having a new glass put in its frame. I took the call saying it was ready, so I just collected it and put it in here rather than tell him about it and open up all the pain again.' She closed the drawer and looked at Clare. 'I'm sorry about all that. Now, is there anything else you need?'

'Nothing, I'm sure. You've thought of everything.'

'Then I'll leave you for the moment.'

After the housekeeper had gone, Clare stood looking round the room with its forget-me-not wallpaper and matching fabrics. The bed was a small four-poster and the wardrobe and dressing-table were antique, delicate and gleaming with years of polishing.

She opened up both her cases, deciding that while it was no use hanging anything up, since it would only have to be folded again and repacked before she went to bed, she could at least sort out what she would need in Italy and what could be left here to collect on her return.

For the first time she felt more at ease about the next two weeks. Somehow what Mrs Kaye had told her made Adam seem more human, more understandable.

The cases sorted out, Clare left them on the bed and went to freshen up in the bathroom. It was still only seven-fifteen. Through the open window of the bedroom the multitude of greens from the garden called her. She decided that she couldn't quite bring herself to go and pour out Mr Melvin's drinks in spite of his invitation, but there was nothing to stop her looking round his grounds. She exchanged the jacket of her suit for a cream sweater, her high-heeled shoes for flat sandals, and went downstairs and out into the courtyard.

There were white doves up on the mossy tiles of the roof, their cooing friendly and conspiratorial. Looking around her, Clare walked over the little bridge that crossed the moat and led to the main garden. On the left was a long wall that zigzagged sharply down the length of the lawn. A crinkle-crankle wall . . . she remembered the name with pleasure. There were espalier fruit trees set in its angles to catch the full benefit of the sun. Clare walked alongside it to the far end of the garden, and by standing on the maintaining wall of the herbaceous border she could see over the garden wall and into the field beyond. There were traces of ruins there, some stones visible, others just grassy mounds—the remains, perhaps, of the original Friary from which the house had taken its name, she guessed.

She retraced her steps and stood leaning on the parapet of the bridge, looking down into the still brown water of the moat. A swan came sailing round the corner of the house, followed by a troop of five cygnets. They moved silently in formation under the little bridge, leaving the water restless and stirred. As it cleared, Clare saw the reflection of a face beside her own, and, startled, turned to see that Adam Melvin was standing behind her.

'As alarming as that, am I?' His eyebrows slanted a sardonic accompaniment to the question.

'You are when you imitate a spirit of the deep. I saw your reflection in the water,' she explained, feeling herself start to blush at her lack of control, and regretting the dissipation of the calm induced by the lovely garden.

'This spirit eats——' he said, 'and I'm told dinner's ready. We'd better go and have it. I've still got things to do afterwards. I presume you don't mind amusing yourself?'

'Of course not. You have a beautiful house and garden.'

'Wander round the rest of the building after dinner if you like. Mrs Kaye has keys hanging in the kitchen—they're all labelled. I can't do the honours myself.'

Mrs Kaye saw that they were amply served with asparagus soup, pointed out the chicken casserole and vegetables on the hot plate, and the raspberry mousse on the sideboard with the coffee things, then announced that she would leave them to it.

'Not going to bed early, I hope?' Adam asked her. 'I'm going to go over the lawns after dinner, and you know what a racket that thing makes.'

'No, I'm not going to bed. There's a serial I'm watching on television. I'll clear up after that. Though why you can't leave the lawns to the man who's supposed to do them when he comes in next week instead of rushing around before you go away, I really don't know, Mr Melvin,' the housekeeper told him with the familiarity of long acquaintance.

'If a damned mowing machine's the only thing I can drive at the moment, I'm blowed if I'll hand that over to someone else,' Adam said pithily. 'Good soup—but that's no surprise.' He nodded his approval of the delicious smell rising from his bowl. Mrs Kaye managed both to cluck her disapproval and smile her thanks simultaneously, and withdrew.

For a short while Adam and Clare ate in silence. He had changed, she noticed, from his office suit into jeans and a white sweat-shirt which emphasised his darkness. He finished his soup well ahead of her and sat back staring thoughtfully at her across the table.

'Tell me why a competent secretary like you is wandering around doing footling jobs and filling in for other people instead of climbing a promotional ladder in some yuppie firm or other,' he said eventually.

'That's a fairly long story, Mr Melvin,' Clare said.

'All right—we've still got a lot of eating to do. And there's no need to 'Mr Melvin' me like some nervous schoolgirl, for heaven's sake!'

'Would you prefer "sir"?' Clare countered with a grin.

He returned it briefly. 'When the occasion arises. For the next two weeks "Adam" will be just as quick and rather less formal. So . . . why are you temping?'

Clare fought the dangerous stir of feelings that she had neither fully expressed nor come to terms with since her mother died. It was just five weeks ago. She could think the words now, but she wasn't yet up to talking about it with self-possession. Indeed, she didn't want to talk about it at all. But she was aware that she had to get over this cramping emotion that had such a grip on her, or she could end up warped by it.

'Well . . .' she began slowly, 'in the first place I never meant to be a secretary. I had every intention of going to university to read English. In fact, I stayed on for a second year in the Upper Sixth so that I could try for Oxford or Cambridge. They thought I had a chance.'

'And were they over-optimistic?'

'No—I got a place, but I didn't take it up.'

'That sounds ridiculously wasteful. Why not?'

She swallowed. Go on, she told herself. Get it over with. 'My mother became ill, and I decided I was needed at home. My father had his own business to run. He couldn't act as nurse and do that.' And her father had always been a man for whom business took precedence, but she wasn't going to tell Adam Melvin that.

'So you became the dutiful daughter. No, I'm not implying that you shouldn't have done so.' He had caught the flash of steel in Clare's grey eyes at his unfortunate phrasing. 'Loyalty is something I admire. I'm just curious to know how the secretary bit came into it.'

'My mother——' It was painful every time she said the words, but presumably there would be a point way ahead in the future when that would change. 'My mother was very concerned that I was spending so much time with her. Sometimes she had quite good days and she felt it was a waste. So my father suggested I got myself decent shorthand-typing speeds, then he'd find part-time work for me in his business when circumstances allowed. I thought that both skills would come in useful in the future, and if I needed to be at home Dad would of course agree to it. It seemed a sensible idea, and it made Mother feel better. My father publishes children's books. Eventually I did quite a bit of proof-checking for him as well—that could always be done at home. It worked out quite satisfactorily.'

Apart from the fact that it was working in the family business that had thrown her so much into Giles's company. But that was another story, and certainly one that she had no intention of starting to tell.

'Obviously things are better now at home?'

Clare went over to get the chicken casserole, glad of the chance to conceal her face. Glad too of the wrong assumption.

'Oh, yes,' she lied brightly. 'Fine now.' She couldn't say the words to this man—even less now that Mrs Kaye had talked to her about his own sadness. It was all too raw, too involved, for both of them.

'Why didn't you consider taking up your place at university at this point, then?' he went on.

'Because—oh, I don't know. Because I'm a different person, now. Older. I can't go back to that point. It was two years ago.'

'Old, at—what are you? An extra year in the Sixth—twenty-one? Twenty-two? Such sad maturity!'

Sad maturity . . . it seemed a strangely apt description of her state of mind.

'I suppose I felt I'd like to wander a bit,' she said after a moment.

'A little further than you anticipated!'

'Yes.' She seized the change of subject thankfully. 'Yes! Tell me about this film. What exactly will you be doing?'

Adam Melvin looked at his watch, brought back to tomorrow's departure after his burst of curiosity about her. 'Good lord, is it as late as that? We'd better get on with this meal. I can't sit here all night talking,' he said accusingly, as though it was her fault. 'I'll tell you anything you need to know on the plane tomorrow. Do help yourself to vegetables.'

He was the one who had initiated the discussion, Clare thought as she flashed a slightly piqued look at his glossy head, lowered over his plate as he ate heartily. By taking judiciously small helpings she managed to keep pace with him to the end of the meal. When he had poured the coffee he creamed his own so that he could drink it at one go, and disappeared with a brief excuse into the grounds.

Clare had a second coffee and a large second helping of raspberry mousse to enjoy in peace, then she cleared the table and left the dishes neatly stacked in the kitchen, knowing instinctively that Mrs Kaye would not like her to do more.

She took advantage of Adam's suggestion that she should look round the house. It appealed to her enormously. Even the dusty quietness of the closed-off area had its silent charm, and the maze of staircases and low-ceilinged rooms seemed to speak happiness to her, although she knew that that happiness could not have been unbroken. Monk's Eden, though, seemed to have the strength to absorb all that had happened within its walls and impose its own age-old calm.

Eventually Clare took the keys back to the kitchen and faced up to something she knew she had to do. She had to phone her father. He couldn't be left in ignorance of what had happened to her. Certainly she couldn't go abroad without letting him know that she would be out of the country. She didn't look forward to speaking to him—she would have preferred to pass on the information by remote control through the post, but she felt duty-bound to do the thing personally. He, like herself, she supposed, had been acting under stress of bereavement over the past weeks, and though she couldn't and wouldn't allow him to ruin her life with his dominance, she didn't want to hurt and worry him more than necessary.

She decided to walk into Lavenham and find a public callbox. It wasn't likely to be the kind of conversation she would be happy to have anyone walk in on.

Out in the grounds Adam was just getting off the ride-on mower to empty the cuttings box, and the sound of the motor covered her approach. He had stripped off his white sweat-shirt, and as he stooped to unfix the box and swing it up to empty the grass on to the compost heap Clare watched him in frank admiration. He had a superb body, spare-fleshed, well-muscled, with broad shoulders tapering to a firm waist. She realised as she watched the movement of muscles under the smooth, tanned skin that she had never seen Giles in a similar state of undress. Giles had not been over-fond of physical activity, describing sport as a mindless waste of time and manual work as something for others to occupy themselves with. Giles would run to fat in time, that was obvious. Already there were signs of it, and his fair, rather pallid colouring would not stand comparison with the dark, bronzed man she was watching now.

That's unnecessarily unkind, she rebuked herself. Giles belongs to the past. Let him stay there.

Adam saw her as he turned to come back to the mower, and walked over to her. With something of an effort she managed to keep her eyes on his face, glad that her thoughts were not available to him.

'All right?' he asked.

'Fine. I'm going to have a little walk before it gets dark.'

He had taken a handkerchief from the pocket of his jeans and was mopping his glistening forehead and neck. Clare's eyes, against her better judgement, followed the movement of the handkerchief.

'Did you look round the house?' he asked.

'I did. What a fascinating maze of a building it is! A wonderful place for children.'

It was being distracted by the sheer animal beauty of him that drew such a cruelly inappropriate comment from her, and Clare would have given anything to be able to take back her unfortunate words, but apart from a slight veiling of his eyes as he looked at her there was no open reaction.

'So I've been told. Don't get lost, will you?'

'I won't.' Thankfully she turned away and went back over the bridge towards the arch leading to the road.

Her own discomfort served her right for being so impressionable, but any hurt she had inflicted on Adam was to be regretted. Perhaps she had triggered off a chain of memories for him now. The thought irked her as she walked towards Lavenham through lanes heavy with the evening scent of flowering hedgerows. Then the sight of a phone-box brought different apprehension about the call she was going to make.

'Clare!' Her father's voice exploded in her ear. 'I've been out of my mind with worry. What made you do such a crazy thing? Where are you, for heaven's sake? Giles has only just left. Have you tried to phone him? The poor chap doesn't know what's hit him. Clare, how could you?'

Clare selected one question from the volley he had fired at her.

'There really was nothing else I could do. I tried to talk to you, and to Giles, so many times, but you wouldn't listen, either of you.'

Nor was her father listening now. 'You're acting under stress, Clare. It's been a hard time for all of us. Come home and give yourself the chance to calm down.'

'Daddy, I *am* calm. And I am entirely myself. The time when I wasn't in my right mind was when I let myself get so involved with Giles.'

'That's utter nonsense! There couldn't be a more suitable man for you than Giles. I won't hear a word against him.'

'I don't want a *suitable* man,' Clare said passionately. 'I want a man I love. And I don't love Giles. Oh, he was kind while Mummy was ill. It was comforting to have him around, and from your point of view my marrying your partner was ideal. I know that it pleased Mummy to feel that my future was taken care of, and anything that made her feel a little better seemed good at the time. But I should never have let things go so far. I blame myself for that. But I'd blame myself even more if I went on into a marriage that would never work. I'm sorry, Daddy, really I am, but I'm not coming back. Not yet. Not until I'm really sure you accept that I mean what I say.'

There was a silence, then her father asked, 'Where are you?'

Clare bit her lip, then apologised again. 'I'm sorry, but I'm not going to tell you. You'd only do everything in your power to get me back to Walberswick, or send Giles to do it—and it just wouldn't get us anywhere, I promise you. Tomorrow, in any case, I shall be out of the country on a job for a fortnight. I'll phone you as soon as we're back. I hope . . . well, I hope you'll understand by that time.'

'"We"? Who the hell do you mean by "we"?' her father barked.

'Sorry, I've no more change, Daddy. Giles will be all right. I was only "suitable" for him, too. Goodbye.'

Clare put down the receiver, cutting off her father at the start of another attempt to make her change her mind. She had phoned him, but she didn't know what she had achieved by doing so. She felt emotionally exhausted as she walked back through the scented dusk along the quiet road to Monk's Eden.

She hoped to be able to slip upstairs to her own room without seeing anyone, but Adam Melvin was in the study when she came back into the house. He looked up as she passed the open door, the lamplight casting shadows that emphasised the strong lines of his face.

'Can I offer you a nightcap?' he asked. 'You've been rather a neglected guest, I'm afraid.'

'Thanks, but I think I'll go straight up,' said Clare.

'You could help yourself to a milky drink if you prefer it. Mrs Kaye's gone to her quarters again, but the kitchen is easy enough to find your way around.'

'No, really, I'm fine. If you have a road atlas handy I'll have a look at the route to Gatwick tomorrow.'

He went over and took a book from the shelves. 'No need, really, I know the way well enough. However, if you feel you must . . .'

Clare looked at the still laden desk. 'Is there anything I can do to help?'

'No—thanks all the same. Just a few personal matters to attend to. Got everything you need?'

'And more! Well, if there's nothing you need me for . . .' Clare was hovering awkwardly instead of briskly going on her way, some kind of magnetism holding her in his presence, though her mind was telling her to go.

'Sure you won't change your mind about a drink?' He was half smiling down at her as though knowing the effect he was having on her and amused by it.

Clare made the necessary effort and backed towards the door.

'Absolutely sure. Goodnight, then.'

'Up at seven. Mrs Kaye will bring you tea. Goodnight, Clare.'

On the way upstairs Clare found herself picturing how different that little scene would have been if his wife, the lovely girl in the picture, had gone into the shadowy study. She would have leaned across the desk and kissed him, persuaded him away from his work and made him come whispering and laughing up the stairs with her, her arm round his waist, her head on his shoulder . . .

What is the matter with you? she asked herself crossly.

The open cases on her bed brought her back to practicalities. The one she was leaving behind ought to be locked, she supposed. She opened her purse to take out the key from the little zipped compartment where she kept it, and there, gleaming at her, was Giles's ring.

'Damn—oh, damn!' she swore softly.

When she had written him her hurried goodbye, she had meant to leave the ring with the note at her father's house—had indeed said as much. But somehow in the heat of the moment, strung up as she was, she had forgotten to do just that. It was not until she was on the London train that she had realised she was still wearing the ring and had taken it off.

She turned it over in her fingers now. It was a dreadful ring, in her opinion. A square-cut yellow diamond, it must have cost the earth, but it was as unfeeling and as meaningless as the relationship it represented. Vulgar, even, Clare thought it. She had not been consulted about it, and Giles had even had his own initials engraved inside it. He had not even done her the courtesy of adding her own, merely remarking that it pleased him to think of her going around with his mark on her. He had no doubt thought that romantic. It was sure to be heavily insured in his name, too, but even so she didn't want the responsibility of taking it around Italy with her.

If she asked Adam to put it in his safe, though, that would mean explaining about Giles. And why should she have to get involved in that?

She made up her mind and went over to the spare case. She tucked the ring under some winter tights and handkerchiefs in the elasticated pocket—she seemed to have brought everything but the kitchen sink—then locked the case securely, putting the key back in her purse. It would all be safe enough here.

Perhaps it was thinking of Giles and the unsatisfactory time with him that made her go over to the chest of drawers and take out the photograph of Adam's wife again. She stood looking down at the smiling face with its revealing expression . . .

The door catch must not have caught properly, because she thought she had closed it. Adam's voice sent a stab of shame and panic through Clare as she looked up, horrified to see him standing in the doorway.

'There you are. I realised after you'd gone——' he began, then he saw the silver frame in her hands and his voice stopped suddenly, changed completely in tone when he went on, 'What's that?'

Clare held out the frame in silence. There was no explanation she could give that would not involve Mrs Kaye in awkwardness. He took it from her and she said, 'I'm sorry . . .' her voice shaky with emotion. Every fibre of her being was aware of his reaction. She saw the tiny movement of the muscle of his jaw clench as he looked down at the face of his wife. She felt that she could sense his breathing change, his heartbeat alter. The temperature in the room fell in an instant, she was sure. 'It was in one of the drawers . . .' Her voice faltered into silence.

'And you were curious.' His eyes were cold and

without feeling as he looked at her. 'You will have to remain so. Your concern is with the present, not the past.' He threw another road map on the bed. 'I gave you an out-of-date map book. This is current.'

Without another word, he turned and left the room, taking the picture with him and closing the door with such unnatural quietness that Clare knew he was resisting the desire to slam it and shout his anger and pain at this intrusion into his past life.

She ached with humiliation. She had her bath and washed and dried her hair. She sat in bed studying the map book, and still her cheeks felt as if they were burning with shame.

She got out of bed and went over to the window. Leaning out, she tried to absorb some calm from the garden in the moonlight. It was several moments before she tore her eyes away from the silhouettes of the lovely trees and looked directly down into the moat. Bright patterns from the windows of the house lay on the dark water. Nearest the wall beneath her was the light from the sitting-room, the room directly below her own—not a solid oblong of light . . . there was the unmistakable shadow of Adam centred in it. He must be standing looking out of the window as she was.

She leaned on the sill, waiting to see him move. Then she realised that above the shape of his window lay the smaller square of her own, with her own silhouette as unmistakable as Adam's.

Clare gulped. Perhaps he was even staring at her reflection as she was staring at his, catching her apparently snooping again. She straightened up and hurriedly began to close the window and withdraw, but not before she saw his shadow raise its arms and draw the curtains, leaving the waters of the moat black where there had been brightness.

She didn't blame him. She would have done the same.

CHAPTER THREE

MORNING dawned capriciously dull and showery, and by the time everyone was stirring the rain had settled into a steady downpour.

Adam seemed withdrawn. He had breakfasted before Clare. If there hadn't been the unfortunate incident of the previous night, she would have put his manner down to simple preoccupation with the mechanics of getting off. Now she wondered if he resented her presence and wished he had never got involved with her, but at least nothing overt was said. Mrs Kaye's innocently unaware, cheerful presence eased things along, and at least all the luggage was stowed and the two of them were on their way, with Clare sensing that the fact that she was in what Adam considered his rightful place behind the steering wheel did nothing to help matters.

'Take the B1071, then the 1115 as far as Sudbury,' he said as they turned out into the road.

'And then the A131? It's a good straight Roman road. That will take us to Chelmsford where we join the A12. After that it's easy, isn't it? The M25 to junction 7, then the M23 to the Gatwick turn-off.'

'I suppose that's as quick a way as any of saying 'Sit back and don't interfere',' Adam said drily.

'No, it's not!' Clare protested. 'I was just telling you I'd thought it out.'

He glanced sideways at her and she felt it.

'My dear girl, it would never have occurred to me

to imagine that your research wouldn't have been absolutely meticulous.'

Was that a dig about last night and the photograph? Clare attempted a move away from dangerous ground.

'Pity about the rain . . .' But he had slumped down in his seat, head back, eyes closed. So be like that, she said inwardly, and concentrated on her driving.

'Which car park is it?' she asked as they neared Gatwick.

'Glad to know I can be of use,' he said, proceeding to tell her. Clare ignored the sarcasm, telling herself that the most angelic of men, she supposed, would hate to be in his position, and Adam Melvin was certainly no angel.

He was a very handsome devil, though, she thought as she followed his progress over to the desk in the departure lounge. He was wearing a beige lightweight suit, beautifully cut and discreetly expensive-looking, and he was wearing it well. His dark, glossy hair was immaculately groomed,and there was easy authority in his stride and approach. The girl on the desk obviously shared Clare's admiration, without the reluctance. She was smiling and making eyes at him while she answered his questions, but with singularly little effect. The detached mood was still in operation here, apparently.

'The flight's on time,' he said briefly when he rejoined Clare. 'It's not worth going into the coffee lounge. We might as well hang on here.'

They waited in silence for a few moments until Adam rose at a voice over the loudspeaker, telling Clare to hurry, for their flight was being called.

She dashed after him with her hand-luggage.

'I thought I heard them say "Palermo",' she said when she caught up with him. 'Are you sure this is the right one?'

There were the first traces of a smile—self-satisfied.

'This part of the journey is my affair. It's your turn to sit back and be blindly propelled towards a destination now.'

He didn't speak again until they were up in the no man's land of the clouds. Clare, who hated take-offs, had closed her eyes until she felt the plane level out and the pressure decrease. When she opened them again, Adam was looking at her.

'So the competent Miss Vincent doesn't care for take-offs. Nice to know somebody else has problems.'

'I don't care for landings either,' Clare told him, unruffled. 'And I don't in the least mind who knows it.' She unfastened her seat belt and smiled at him, determined to get things on a more friendly level. 'But the bit in between's fine.'

Adam picked up his briefcase and balanced it on his lap. 'In that case, I said I'd tell you more about what I'm going to film. I'd better begin by saying that our destination *is* Sicily, not mainland Italy.'

Clare's eyebrows rose. 'So why did you tell me Italy, then?'

'I didn't. If you recall, I merely asked if you'd ever been to Italy. You made the assumption that that was where we were going.'

'As you meant me to!'

'Maybe I thought a slight confusion might be a good thing, just in case, by some fluke, you and John bumped into each other.'

'There wasn't much chance of that. And couldn't

you have relied on my discretion?'

'I prefer to rely on safety rather than trust.'

Clare felt hurt at this, but Adam seemed to attach no great importance to what he had just said. He opened a file that he had taken from his briefcase and went through the papers in it. 'The film we went to Sicily to work on was the final interview in a series of six—all interviews with people whose lives had taken them away from their origins, but who, for one reason or another, had returned towards the end to their place of birth—sometimes against all the odds.'

'So it isn't strictly a travel film either,' Clare observed.

'Yes, it is, but of a rather specialised nature. We show the background in each country a person is involved with, but the main interest is in the psychological journey, if you like. Much more interesting than a straight travel documentary, and a lot more revealing about the place as well as about the person.'

Clare considered a moment, then nodded. 'Yes, I can see that it would be.'

'The whole series will go out under the title *Back to the Roots*. We've done five interviews with ordinary unknowns, selected from answers to our researcher's adverts in the daily papers.'

'And the final one? Who is that to be with?' asked Clare.

Adam selected a clip of papers from the file and passed them to her. 'No need to ask if the name is familiar, I'm sure.'

'Marcella Rafaeli!' Clare's eyes widened. 'I didn't know she was still around. She hasn't made any films for ages—more's the pity.'

'She's in her seventies, I'd guess from the data we

have, but very much alive. She's been back in Sicily for the past three years. She's apparently more or less abandoned the States after spending her life there since her late teens. That's what made us so very interested when, out of the blue, she sent in a rather cryptic reply to the *New York Times* advert. She still has that sent on to her, it seems.'

'Apart from the films of hers that I've seen, which were wonderful, I hardly know anything about her,' Clare said. 'She seems to have shunned publicity of a personal nature all her life, and yet now she's seeking it. No wonder you were intrigued!'

'Even more so when we discovered the reason for her leaving Sicily. She was engaged to someone from the village where she was born, but he died—violently. There were rumours of Mafia connections at the time, but nothing ever came to court—that was par for the course in those days. Marcella left almost at once. As far as we know, she never came back in the years between.'

'But something has taken her back now . . . Did you find out the reason?'

Adam shook his head. 'We'd gone over to talk—that was all she'd agreed to initially, but I took the complete crew because I had a hunch that this might be a case where we had to go full steam ahead the second we got a breakthrough. We'd almost reached that point. Marcella had asked all the questions she had up her sleeve, and seemed to have decided that her story would be handled with dignity and would form a suitable conclusion—the high spot, if you like, of the series.'

'What happened, then?' Clare was so absorbed in what Adam was telling her that she had forgotten where she was. Forgotten too that there had been that slight animosity between them.

A shadow swept across his face. 'Ah—then . . . We had the most unfortunate, sad bad luck. One of the crew had an accident. His car went off the road at a point where the drop and the nature of it—it was a rocky, uneven near-cliff face—meant that he couldn't do a thing to save himself. So we were recalled the instant the sponsors knew what had happened. We were delving into a story—albeit an old one—where Mafia involvement was suspected. Their immediate thought, in spite of my reassurances, was that we were being told—not too subtly—to let the past remain just that.'

'You mean they thought it was murder?'

'They thought the accident was set up, whether murder was the intention or not.' Adam shifted impatiently in his seat. 'It just wasn't like that. We were in two cars, Don first with the equipment, the rest of us following him. We'd got radio phones so that we could stop each other if either of us saw something that struck us as good for background filming. Don was actually speaking to me when it happened. As we came up to a bend, we had a first superb view of Etna. He was saying, "Look at that!" or something, and his eyes were anywhere but on the road.' Adam's voice deepened as he relived the accident.

'It must have been awful . . . And they wouldn't believe you when you told them this?' Clare asked.

'They wouldn't. And the car was such a write-off that there was no chance of proving that it hadn't been tampered with.'

'You lost all the equipment too, I presume?'

'We could have hired more if we'd been allowed to stay on and complete the job.'

Clare looked at him, not quite believing what she was hearing.

'You don't mean you'd have gone on as though nothing had happened there and then? You'd lost a member of the crew—a working colleague, if not a close friend.'

Adam's dark blue eyes returned her stare steadily. 'A damned good working colleague, who would have been the first not to want to see a good opportunity wasted.'

Clare was struck silent by this total commitment to work at the expense of people.

'I suppose you're thinking along the obvious feminine lines now,' he said a touch scathingly. ' "How horrid! How unfeeling!" It's too much to expect a woman to understand a man's world.'

Clare looked her reproach at him. 'Not all men would deny straightforward human feelings about something like that,' she said.

He ignored the criticism. 'Maybe you're even deciding that you're a bit scared . . . wondering if there could possibly be any truth in the sponsors' idea of what happened.' He was looking assessingly at her.

Clare said, 'Tell me something. If there were truth in their idea, would it have stopped you wanting to complete the film? Would you have held back from bringing me out with you?'

Adam rested his head against the seat back and stared up at the ceiling of the plane. 'I've told you, it's too good a story to miss,' he said obliquely. Then suddenly he turned to her again in challenge. 'So what do you say to that? Are you scared? Do you want to chicken out of the whole thing?'

Clare returned his gaze, her grey eyes unwavering.

'I say this: I think your hard-headedness verges on sheer callousness. But I don't want to "chicken out" as you put it. And I'm not in the least scared. If you want to know why, I think you're much too shrewd an operator to risk another "accident" damaging your reputation. You must be pretty sure of your facts, or you wouldn't be bringing anyone else along with you.'

'Is that so?' His head was still turned towards her, his expression unreadable.

She warmed to her own defence. 'It is. And as for being scared of people, that's nonsense. Even if there had been some shady secret in Marcella's past, how long ago is it? Fifty years or more? Whoever was involved is almost certainly dead, I imagine. The whole idea is crazy. No, I'm not in the least scared, you can rest assured.'

'Ready to rush in where angels fear to tread, are you? That doesn't augur well.'

'Well, you can't have it both ways, can you?' Clare said with cheerful reasonableness. 'Either I'm too scared to be of much use to you, or I go blithely on and do the job you've hired me to do.'

'With a modicum of tact and a healthy respect for the metaphorical roof you find yourself under, I hope,' he said.

This time Clare did rise to the unmistakable allusion.

'I know you think badly of me because of last night, and I don't blame you. I apologised then, and I do so again now. I assure you that I shall behave with all the tact in the world while we're in Sicily. What more can I do?'

Adam outstared her for a moment, then he said, 'You can get on with looking through the papers I've given you.' He turned his face away, closing his eyes and folding his arms as he settled down in the seat.

Clare wondered how it was possible to veer from being fascinated by what he was saying, as she had been only moments ago, to feeling, as she did now, that it would be quite satisfying to push him out of the plane and say 'Good riddance!' One moment he was telling her all this interesting background to the filming job, the next he was shutting her up like an importunate schoolgirl and expecting her to obey him without question, just as he had done last night when she'd tried to start talking about the film over dinner.

She began reading the research on Marcella Rafaeli, stopped for a moment when she realised that she was doing exactly as she was told, then decided that it was too interesting to argue or stand on her dignity about and buried her head in the file again.

Bu the time she had finished reading, a glance at Adam showed her that he really had gone to sleep. His chest was rising and falling steadily. Clare carefully edged round sideways against the window so that she could stare at him in comfort.

Asleep, he looked quite different. The dark lashes against his cheeks gave a trace of vulnerability to the face that was so tough in wakefulness, and the impatient lines were smoothed out into a deceptive serenity. Yes, Clare thought, I could quite like him if he stayed like this. He looks a bit of a pussy-cat. Must look positively sweet in bed!

She was beginning to smile at the thought when the pussy-cat opened one eye and growled 'Now what?' startling her into dropping the file, retrieving the contents of which neatly got her out of the need to answer him. The arrival of the stewardess with refreshments extended the diversion, and the flight continued for the remaining two hours with no further incidents.

When they landed at Punta Raisi airport, Adam left Clare to guard the luggage while he went off to make enquiries about the car he had hired. All was confusion in the lounge, with two large tour parties whose take-off was delayed volubly bemoaning their misfortune.

Clare was thoroughly enjoying the wholehearted expression of annoyance and thinking how different it was from the depressed silence of an English crowd in similar circumstances, when someone came up behind her and whispered an incomprehensible but—to judge by the tone of voice—unmistakably naughty suggestion in her ear.

She turned to see a good-looking young man whom she assumed to be Sicilian, his dark eyes flashing admiration at her, his face expressing a mixture of boyish admiration and wariness of her reaction.

He looked so comical that she laughed, and he took her laughter for encouragement, breaking into a flood of Italian, French, and very broken English while he tried to establish her nationality and pay her compliments that ranged, according to his gestures, from the colour and shininess of the fall of her hair to the snug fit of her pink cat-suit.

Clare decided that he was harmless and the place public enough for her not to overreact, and she stood her ground, quietly smiling while he got on with his performance.

Adam, coming back from the car-hire desk, took no such tolerant view of things. Clare was startled to feel his hand with a light but possessive touch rest on her shoulder as he looked at the boy and asked in traditional stage-heavy style, 'Is this man bothering you, darling?'

Whether the youth understood the words in their entirety or not, he certainly got the message. He disappeared into the crowd like lightning.

When she had recovered from the surprise of the 'darling', Clare said, 'You needn't have done that. He was harmless enough.'

'How do you know?' It was obvious that Adam was displeased. 'How do you know what lewd things he might have been saying about you—for the entertainment of everyone within earshot?'

Clare moved so that his hand fell to his side.

'He was only a boy having a bit of innocent fun.'

Adam snorted impatiently. 'I'd like to see a Sicilian's reaction if somebody chatted up one of his women in that kind of way!'

Her hackes rose. 'This should be an unnecessary reminder—but I don't happen to *be* one of your women, do I? And as a matter of fact, I strongly object to your behaving as though I were.'

He was walking at a pace Clare had difficulty in keeping up with towards the point where they would be able to pick up the car.

'If that is an example of the discreet behaviour you spoke of on the plane,' Adam said coolly, 'may I suggest that you have a fair way to go in that respect.' His face was blandly calm so that no one would have known that a rather vitriolic exchange was taking place. 'Perhaps I should also point out that, as you are *one of the women* I am currently employing, everything you say and do reflects on me.'

He broke off to speak to the uniformed car hire representative, leaving Clare speechless with annoyance at being made to feel she was some kind of chattel, and an ill-behaved onc at that.

'Do you realise—' he went on as though there had been no hiatus once they were sitting in the Fiat '—that in some of the lesser villages girls are still guarded like priceless possessions? Marriages are arranged, and courtships conducted according to a careful, centuries-old pattern, so elaborate that you'd never understand it.'

'Look,' said Clare in expasperation, 'people are people the world over. And this isn't exactly the back of beyond—it's a lovely island that tourists happen to flock to in their thousands. I think I'll manage not to put my foot in it too many times. And now, if you don't mind, I'd like to concentrate on starting up what is after all the second strange car of the day. I can do it, don't worry, but I prefer to think about it rather than go into the social anthropology of Sicily, fascinating though it may be.'

'Lord!' Adam exploded. 'If only I could drive myself!'

'Amen to that!' Clare retorted smartly. 'If you could, I wouldn't need to be here!' The engine roared as her temper reached the accelerator. 'Where to?' she asked crisply, going on without giving Adam a chance to answer, 'I am not normally a rude person. I hate the way you seem to be turning me into one.'

He was trying to accommodate his long legs in the small car, and finally succeeded in adjusting the seat to his satisfaction. 'Palermo. Follow the signs—you can't go wrong. I'll tell you when we're nearer. Just concentrate on not crashing us.'

After that shot, he restrained himself and actually

let Clare get on with the job. The thirty kilometres passed in silence quite smoothly, and though it was rather hair-raising when they came to the capital, Adam was familiar enough with Palermo from his recent visit to be able to direct her to a possible parking place without too much hesitation.

He was looking quite calm again, she noticed when she risked a quick glance as she switched off the engine. The heat of the sun was very noticeable through the open car windows now that they were not benefiting from the breeze of movement. Adam actually grinned at her.

'You can attribute a lot of blame to air travel and hot climates,' he said. She supposed that was his idea of an apology. 'There are one or two things I have to attend to here,' he went on, 'and I'll be quicker on my own. Wait in the car a second—I'm not really off yet.' He disappeared, leaving Clare looking around her with fascination.

She had half expected to be surrounded by dark hair and eyes and to stand out as a foreigner with her light golden-brown hair, but she could see indications of many different lines of ancestry in the people who were passing by. There were classical Greek profiles, examples of the kind of beauty reminiscent of Arab races, and even a sprinkling of Norman fair hair and blue eyes. The part of the capital where they had parked had a fair proportion of old buildings, some of them very beautiful, and Clare itched to explore.

She saw Adam coming back and got out to lock the car in anticipation of a few minutes' peaceful wandering.

'I thought you might be interested to look round the Cappuccini Monastery while you're waiting.

There may not be another chance,' he said, handing her a ticket. 'There you are. By the time you've done that, I'll be back and waiting here. The entrance is just along to the right.'

Clare took the ticket, her smile dazzling him as she reacted to this unexpected gesture.

'That's kind of you, Adam. I was just wishing I could wander round a bit. Thank you very much.'

'I'll be waiting,' he repeated. 'Make sure you take in the whole tour. You'll find it fascinating.'

Perhaps this was his way of really apologising for his high-handedness, Clare thought as she walked down towards the monastery. She was slowly beginning to get the measure of the man, she felt. As Mrs Kaye had said, his abrupt manner was capable of hiding occasional kindnesses. Clare wondered if he had sent champagne to the man who ought to have been with him right now, and whom he had cursed so roundly yesterday. She rather thought he would have done.

As the tour of the monastery began, she felt quite warm towards Adam Melvin. By the time it concluded—prematurely for her—she had had her feelings drastically changed.

The last part of the tour was horrifyingly unexpected. She followed the small crowd of sightseers in all innocence into the catacombs without realising where she was going.

Suddenly she found herself surrounded by the most spine-chilling collection of human remains. There was the body of a child, no more than five years old, women and men of all ages—and all of them dressed as though they were still alive, their faces still covered with a leathery mockery of flesh but their expressions distorted so that they seemed to portray utter anguish.

'Preserved!' the woman in front of Clare turned to say carefully, proud of her vocabulary. She had performed a stumbling but valiant translation service all the way round. Clare managed to nod, willing the woman to turn away again.

The crowd edged slowly on, exclaiming and chattering at each gruesome sight, seeming not exactly unmoved by what they were seeing, but more excited than devastated as Clare was.

She felt sick, faint, panic-stricken. She knew why she was reacting as she was, and the effort not to think of her mother made her heart swell and race, her throat tighten until she thought she would choke. She let everyone pass her, keeping her eyes glued to the hem of the little girl's garment as though she were counting every stitch in the fabric.

Then, when nobody saw, she turned and stumbled blindly out of the catacombs, feeling the sweat stand out on her forehead and dampen the palms of her hands. Outside in the dazzling sunshine, with the sounds of the city coming to her, she leaned against the warm stone wall until the waves of nausea faded and she began to come round.

No one spoke to her. She couldn't have answered if they had done so. Why had Adam sent her into that awful place? To show her how very alien some aspects of another country's past could be? To warn her that she really was in a different world here, one that she must treat with respect? Or had he simply—as it had appeared—sought to pass the time for her while he conducted his business, but in a place the impact of which on her he couldn't possibly have known about? In all fairness, she had to incline towards the latter view.

She began to walk, tentatively at first, her legs feeling alien and unreliable. Then, as she came nearer to the place where they had parked, her step strengthened along with her will and she held her head erect. Bloody but unbowed, she thought, feeling rather feverish.

Adam was leaning on the car, watching her approach.

'OK?' he said casually.

'Fine.' Clare went round to the driver's door and unlocked it, leaning over to release the catch on his side. He loaded a video and screen into the boot, then got in beside her.

'Did you find the Cappuccini interesting?' he asked.

'Very.'

He looked more closely at her. 'Are you all right? You look a bit pale.'

'Do I? As you said, put it down to the heat.' She switched on the engine, and he reached over instantly and turned it off again.

'Are you sure you're all right to drive?' he emphasised.

Clare stared straight ahead, willing herself not to turn and meet the keen look she could feel burning her face. 'Why ever shouldn't I be?' She switched on the engine again.

'There's no almighty hurry, for heaven's sake!' he protested, appearing to be needled by her calmness.

Clare reversed the car smoothly out of its parking space, and he told her to follow the autostrada signs in the direction of Castellammare Trapani.

It took all Clare's concentration to get them safely out of the capital. Adam vouchsafed a brief 'Well done!' as they joined the autostrada. Apart from a businesslike, 'Straight ahead for the next fifty kilometres,' and her equally crisp, 'Right,' they exchanged no further words.

The acacia trees lining the autostrada flashed past in spectacular outbursts of yellow fireworks. Clare began gradually to switch from her inner seething and take in the countryside they were passing through. Mountains and fields, with here and there the flash of a river with the sun on it. Wheatfields ablaze with a lavish dusting of poppies, and on the rough ground here and there a sea of something blue. She would have liked to ask what it was, but she didn't really feel like talking yet.

'Take the Castellammare road, coming up soon,' Adam told her eventually, then later, as they crested the hilltop and saw the corkscrewing descent into the town, he suddenly told her to pull in to the side for a moment.

They sat looking down on the town, built around two small bays, its harbour in the most westerly one. On the cliff promontory between the bays was the castle from which the town got its name.

'Quite a view,' Adam said.

'Yes, quite a view,' Clare echoed.

He spoke irritably. 'Are you going to sulk much longer?'

'Sulk? Why should I be sulking?' Clare asked with polite surprise.

'Oh, don't let's play games. You looked sick as a parrot when you came back from the Cappuccini. Ghastly, in fact. How was I to know you were as sensitive as all that?'

'I'm perfectly all right now,' Clare said calmly. She hoped she was.

'I thought you'd find it interesting. The Cappuccini is unique—not the sort of place you see anywhere else.'

'I'm sure that's true,' she said, suppressing a shudder. 'I'm rather thankful.'

Adam sighed impatiently. 'I had no wish to make you feel ill. But you aren't in a little Suffolk backwater now, you know, among people you've been tuned into from birth. You're on the territory of people with a history and culture you know precious little about. Perhaps it's not to be regretted that you should be shocked into awareness of that—though I don't want this job we're on to be held up too many times while you cope with the vapours.'

'Ah, the job!' Clare said with delicate venom. 'What are we doing admiring a view when there's a job to be done?' She started up the car again and began the descent to Castellammare.

'The next two weeks should be quite interesting,' said Adam, adding with a touch too much emphasis, 'I hope.'

'No doubt they'll be what we manage to make them,' Clare said sweetly, and on that note they both seemed to make a tacit agreement to hold their fire.

CHAPTER FOUR

PAST Castellammare the road grew more quiet, and when they turned off at a sign pointing to San Paolo di Sopra—their destination, Adam, said—it became not much more than a track clinging in places precariously to the side of a rocky headland. Picturing its position on the map, Clare realised that they must be in the most north-westerly tip of Sicily, an area renowned in the past as the haunt of smugglers, but with sunlight dazzling on the water peaceful enough now, if rugged.

As they entered the village, the cobbled streets reduced them to little more than walking pace.

'Stop a minute!' Adam said in the quiet village square. Once the engine was turned off, they could hear the plunking sound of the water that spilled over from basin to basin of the simple stone fountain. The houses were shuttered against the sun, only a dark open doorway here and there indicating the presence of people.

As they looked, a little girl ran out from one of the houses, intent on where she was going, ignoring their presence, and holding a hen upside down by its feet. She went straight over to the fountain and plunged the protesting bird in it for a moment, then held it aloft, dripping and squawking, berating it as she ran back to the house.

Clare had, herself, given a little squawk of surprise.

Adam allowed himself a mini-smile. 'Broody, I

expect. They believe in the short, sharp shock treatment here. Ah, I see where we're supposed to go now. Take the gap between the white house and the ochre one, would you?'

'It doesn't look much like the approach to a hotel,' Clare remarked after a moment as the car jolted and lurched over the uneven stones.

'No reason why it should. Stop here.'

He made her draw up in front of the house, white-walled, the painted shutters a soft, faded blue. Before she could speak, he was out of the car and unlocking the door, then going in and reappearing briefly in window after window as he flung the shutters wide and secured them.

Clare got out herself and followed him into the house in silence. This was something she had not expected. She had assumed, though he had never said as much, she realised now, that they would be staying in a hotel among other people.

Adam passed her, going back to the car to unload their cases, offering neither excuse nor explanation. Clare wandered around the terrazzo-tiled rooms of the ground floor, sizzling with thoughts. The house was unexpectedly roomy and well furnished —nothing to complain about there. When she looked out of the windows at the back, she drew in her breath. There was a small garden, stone-flagged, with flowers and bushes round the borders. A stone wall, its crannies bright with rock plants, ran across the bottom of the garden . . . then nothing. They were perched on the side of the headland, and below them, a long, long way below, was the sea.

'Want to come up and choose a room?' Adam stood in the doorway of the sitting-room, carrying the last of the luggage.

Clare followed him up the stairs. 'This is another thing you didn't tell me,' she said to his back.

He paused on the landing. 'What? The house? No point, was there? I should have been sharing it with Ian Forrester, of course—and it was too late to do anything about the arrangements. Does it bother you?'

She hesitated. 'It might just have been a factor for consideration if I'd known.'

His dark eyes revealed a trace of mockery. 'You needn't worry, I have no evil intent.'

'That idea didn't enter my head,' she said crushingly. 'It was the social intimacy, not the physical, I was thinking about actually.'

'If that's the problem, it would have been one anywhere.'

'But there would have been other people around. However . . .' Clare shrugged and walked into each of the two bedrooms. Both ran from front to back of the house. One had an en-suite shower-room with a vanity unit and loo. The other had no such facilities, depending on the tiny bathroom beyond the stairs. 'I'll take the one with the shower, if that's all right by you,' she said, her eyes defying him to accuse her of choosing the better of the two.

'Right.' He dropped her cases indifferently and left. She heard him close the door of the other room, bang about a bit, then after a while take the stairs down two or more at a time.

By then Clare was unpacking, her mind darting from one implication to another as she thought of the two weeks in San Paolo. She had not been entirely honest about her reaction to sharing the house with Adam. It wasn't just the fear of personality conflict that remained in her thoughts now. It was a strange reluctance to find herself stuck with the prospect of being so much in his physical presence. She shied away from too close an analysis of the reasons for her attitude. He had said—very rudely—that the fact that she was a woman didn't matter in the least to him. She frowned. The only gender-linked idea likely to be in his mind right now was how jolly useful she was likely to be when it came to cooking, washing dishes, and cleaning.

That potential floating grievance was scuppered the minute she walked into the kitchen. Adam was chopping peppers, tomatoes and onions into a saucepan, surrounded by jars of herbs and seasonings on the table.

'Fresh orange juice in the jug. Help yourself.' He nodded an indication of its whereabouts. 'I'd asked for stand-by groceries to be bought in. They don't seem to extend much beyond pasta, so I'm making a sauce. Have you many likes and dislikes? We'll eat out mostly once we're settled, but I don't suppose you feel like careering along the motorway again tonight.'

'Pasta's fine. And I eat everything.' Clare, humbled, poured her fruit juice and perched on a stool, watching him and sipping it slowly. Adam had changed into white slacks and a dark blue shirt. There was a striped butcher's apron hanging on the back of the kitchen door, but Adam apparently drew the line at wearing such a thing. 'Do you like cooking?' she asked.

'I wouldn't like not being able to look after myself if necessary. Why? Have you got outmoded ideas about a man's place? Surely not.'

'Certainly not. I just wouldn't have expected the provision of meals to be one of your skills.'

'You haven't tasted the results yet.' He flashed her a quick look from under his devil's eyebrows. 'But I always prefer to be unexpected.'

'I'd noticed that.' Clare watched on in silence. Now that she was being shown how unnecessary she was in the kitchen, paradoxically she was feeling that she ought to be doing something.

'What are you brooding about?' he asked.

Nothing I can tell you about, she thought. 'Nothing much. This house isn't what you'd expect to find in a small village, especially such a remote one, is it? It's quite luxurious.'

'That's because it belongs to a family who emigrated to America. Quite a lot of the houses in this area are empty for the same reason. People hang on to them in case the new country doesn't work out for them. Smartened up like this one, they bring in enough to cover maintenance through summer lettings.' He put the pan on the stove and stood watching it, waiting for the contents to come to the boil.

'Where does Marcella live?' Clare asked.

'That's the main advantage of this place. Come over to the window.' Clare went and stood beside him, looking out on to the track and the sharp slope of the headland. Theirs appeared to be the last house before the rocks took over. 'See that path?' Adam pointed to the right.

'Yes.' It zigzagged up to the top of the rocky incline where it met the vibrant blue of the sky.

'Over the top and down twice as far, almost to sea-level—that's where Marcella lives. If you're not too desperate for food, I'd like to go over right away. You can drive me there so that I arrive looking respectable, and drop me at the house. I'll walk back over the path—it's a ridiculously long way round by road. We have to go right back to the start of the headland and come along parallel to ourselves to a point opposite herc. Ridiculous, but that's the lie of the land.' He went over and turned the ring down to 'simmer' under the saucepan. 'That'll be all right for an hour or so at least. For as long as we want to leave it, in fact.'

'Is Marcella expecting you?' asked Clare.

'No. Nor am I going to give her the chance to say "no" over the phone,' he said decisively. 'It's always easier to twist somebody's arm when you're in their presence.'

'Should I change?' Clare was still wearing the cat-suit she had travelled in.

'Not necessary. I don't want you hanging around. You can push off as soon as you've dropped me.'

Her eyes widened at his rudeness. 'I'll practise reversing so that I can zoom off the instant you set foot on the ground, if you like.'

'Don't be huffy. If you want a good reason for getting out of the way . . . I shall be referring to you as my wife, and I'm not at all sure after what happened at the airport that you would enjoy playing that role.'

No 'if you don't mind'. No explanation. Just a statement of fact.

'You're joking!' Clare said disbelievingly.

'I'm serious.' She should have known that he wasn't a man to joke about anything. 'Last time we came openly to film,' he went on, 'and we had so many "helpful" officials buzzing around and so much paperwork to see to that I don't want to get involved in all that again. Being a harmless holiday couple will be much easier.'

'*That* I can go along with,' said Clare. 'But I don't see why pretending to be married should be necessary.'

'It's not a question of necessity, more a matter of courtesy to the people we'll be living among for the next two weeks. These tiny communities would tend to look askance at our sort of arrangement. It will save any awkwardness if we're a married couple. Be easier on you in the end.'

Clare was sceptical about that. But was it worth another argument? There seemed to have been so much real and potential conflict in the air, and she felt tired at the thought of another verbal marathon.

Adam was taking something from his shirt pocket. 'Try this for size.'

It was a ring . . . a plain gold band. Clare's eyes flew to his face, openly mirroring her protesting thoughts. Surely it wasn't—couldn't be—the ring that had belonged to his wife? That was something she definitely couldn't stomach.

'Where did you get it?' she asked.

'Palermo. Suddenly realised how it would be while I was collecting the keys for the house. There was a jeweller's nearby. Give me your hand.'

Reassured at least on the ring's origins, Clare reluctantly held out her hand. Adam slid the ring on to her finger, his hand pausing on hers as he turned it experimentally, checking it for fit. 'Not bad. You could wrap a bit of cotton round it if it feels too loose.'

The feel of the ring on her finger roused a mass of emotions in Clare. The memory of Giles surfaced a little again with all its background of trouble. But it wasn't just that. Adam's fingers were still holding her own with casual familiarity, but she seemed unable to accept his touch with similar lightness. His act of putting on the ring, with its echoes of the ritual exchange of the wedding service had strangely demoralised her. She might have hit the whole idea squarely on the head then and there had a voice not said tentatively from the open doorway, '*Per favore, signore, signora* . . .'

One of the women from the village was shyly offering a loaf of freshly baked bread, her tolerant smiling and nodding showing that she was totally taken in by the false picture of a doting husband holding the hand of his shy young wife.

That's it, then, Clare thought angrily as Adam spoke to the woman in competent-sounding Italian. I'm Mrs Superman Melvin now, whether I like it or not.

'Such fiddling attention to detail!' she said when the woman had gone, waving her ring hand crossly in his face.

'That's what counts in my profession,' he said, moving to the door. 'Shall we go?'

She felt a fluttering embarrassment when the sun glittered on the ring out of doors. Ridiculous! she chided herself. Actresses wore rings in the course of their stage work, didn't they? It didn't mean a thing. Why should she make such a big affair of it?

Keeping the car on the track along both sides of the headland occupied her mind to the exclusion of all else for the next twenty minutes. They could see Marcella's house from above before the track doubled frighteningly back on itself in a precarious hairpin bend.

'It was part of a *tonnara*,' Adam told her. 'That's a centre where the tuna-fishermen worked from in the breeding season between March and June. They'd have been here now—but there's not quite so much involvement these days, and this particular *tonnara* was sold off. Marcella's house was originally the owner's *palazzo*. The storage buildings and the men's quarters have gone now to make room for her garden.'

The house was squat and fort-like, glistening white in the sunshine in contrast with the savage grey rocks to which it clung. The garden glowed within its sheltering walls with greens and colours, a tribute to the constant attention that must be necessary to coax life from the earth in such an unfavourable position.

'What's that place?' asked Clare, one hand leaving the steering wheel for a second to point to a ruined tower just below the top of the headland.

'A relic of the Saracen occupation, over a thousand years ago. They came after the Romans and before the Normans.'

'A complex history, as I believe you said.'

'I did hint as much.' They had reached the wrought iron gates set in the white walls. 'Right, I'll see you later.'

As soon as Adam was out of the car, Clare, mindful of his instructions, began to reverse into the mind-blowing turning area, misjudgement of which would send the car plummeting over the cliff edge and into the sparkling sea twenty feet below. Her caution meant that she had to shuffle backwards and forwards a couple of times, which enabled her to see through the gates that someone whose bearing suggested that she must be Marcella herself was walking over from the shelter of the wall to greet Adam.

She was smaller than Clare had thought, her walk still beautiful and supple. Her hair, unashamedly silver-grey, was knotted on top of her head, and she wore her simple black skirt and shirt with as much glamour as the designer clothes so often featured in her films.

Just before she managed to get the car pointing back up the track, Clare saw both Adam and Marcella looking in her direction, and Marcella raised a hand in brief greeting.

Clare gave a token wave in return, outwardly smiling, but at the same time fuming inwardly at the thought of Adam referring to her as his wife—which no doubt he had done.

It's only for two weeks, she told herself yet again, wondering how many more times and in how many different circumstances she was going to repeat those words in the coming days.

Back at the house she went upstairs and had a shower, changing into a white halter-necked dress. She looked with more interest, now that she was alone in the house, at her bedroom. The floor was cork-tiled, cool under her bare feet, and shining, and a big glowing kilim rug in shades of gold and russet filled the area at the foot of the bed, contrasting with the black and white mosaic of the American quilt. Three watercolours above the head of the bed were, at a guess, scenes from the locality, with narrow black frames and burnt orange mounts that were the exact colour of the two big decorative cushions on the bed. A pleasant room, Clare thought, different from any she had slept in before with its strong, clean colours.

Downstairs she checked the sauce, the delicious smell of which was making her feel very hungry. She hunted around for crockery and laid the table. Fresh salad things were on the draining board, so she washed and arranged a bowl-full, and put it in the fridge, then she piled fruit in the white dish on a stand in the centre of the table.

The ring caught her eye again. At least there was no need to wear it here. She removed it and put it on the table, then walked out into the garden and sat on the wall watching the boats far out at sea. The sun was going down quite quickly now. It would soon have disappeared behind the headland, shining a little bit longer on Marcella's side. An aeroplane coming in across the sweep of the bay showed her where she and Adam had landed at Punta Raisi, and she followed the line of the coast round past Castellammare—still catching the sun—to the rocky headland where San Paolo di Sopra was rapidly sinking into dusk.

It was not as pleasant perched on the wall now. Clare scrambled down and decided she might as well walk about the village, though there hadn't appeared to be much of it. She could suss out useful shops if there happened to be any.

On the lower side of the village square men were sitting at a café table. They fell silent, not looking at her as she came towards them, but she felt their eyes on her once she had passed, and heard the conversation start up again with one or two smothered bursts of laughter. Her bare shoulders suddenly felt very conspicuous, and she remembered the appearance of the woman who had brought the bread—black clothes, black shawl thrown over her head.

There was a general store down a little alleyway, and a baker's shop in another narrow side-street.

The child they had seen earlier with the hen was over by the fountain. Clare tried an experimental '*Ciao*!' on her, and was rewarded with a quick flashing smile before the girl ran shyly off into the house.

Still feeling at a loose end, Clare decided to go and see if there was any sign of Adam coming back. She had got almost as far as the top of the path before she saw him, not coming towards her, but sitting on a flat rock, looking back down over the far side of the headland. From the set of his shoulders she could tell that all was not well, but that didn't prevent her feeling an absurd surge of pleasure at the sight of him. Being alone in a strange place wasn't much fun.

Her soft-soled sandals had not announced her arrival.

'Hi!' she said tentatively.

He looked round, jolted out of his absorption, frowning.

'Do you have to creep around after me? Surely there was something you could do for half an hour?'

Clare had been feeling genuinely concerned that he might not have managed to fix things to his satisfaction, and she answered apologetically, 'I've done everything I could think of for the meal. I feel rather awkward about things. I wasn't sure that I ought to be lazing around—I am supposed to be working, after all.'

He stood up, his expression softening slightly, and one hand reached out to push back a strand of hair that the breeze had teased forward over her face.

'Ignore the tone of voice. It was more for Marcella than you.'

'I gathered as much.' Clare was strangely shy

again at his touch, and especially this time at the gentleness of it. She looked up into his face. 'What happened, then? Or would you rather not talk about it?'

Adam turned her round to go back down the track, and his hand took her elbow, guiding and steadying her.

'She was quite pleased to see me, for all the good it did. She was certainly friendly enough, but on balance she seems to have come down on the side of not giving an interview.'

'After you've come all this way?'

'I can't blame her for that. I got no go-ahead before I set out. That was a risk I took. She doesn't have to be swayed by it.'

'But you said she'd more or less agreed to take part in your film.'

'Unfortunately the thinking time has tilted the balance in favour of caution. She taught me my first bit of Sicilian to make her point. . . . *Chu cerca lo picchi ntà li cosi trova spinanzi chi rosi* . . . It rather confirms my feeling that there's a poignant story hidden away there.'

The language suited him, Clare thought, sidetracked for a moment. 'What does it mean?' she asked.

'It's rather poetic, really. "The man who looks for reasons finds thorns as well as roses".'

'Implying that your questions could be painful?'

'Seems like it.'

They walked on in silence for a while, then Clare said, 'Say it again, will you?' Adam humoured her, and she repeated the words after him until she too had them by heart.

'I picked up one word, too, before I came to meet

you,' she told him. 'The men at the café were using it quite a lot when I went past: *bona*. Must have been drinking something they appreciated, if my schoolgirl French is anything to go by. What's the matter?'

He was grinning at her. 'I imagine they were looking at the scenery rather than into their glasses!'

'What do you mean?' Clare asked suspiciously, stopping.

' "*Bona*" doesn't just mean "good". It means sexually good. "A bit of all right", in other words.'

'Oh!' The comic self-ridicule on her face made his smile broaden. He eyed her thoughtfully—bare shoulders, slender golden arms and legs, the colour flooding her cheeks . . .

'Don't tell me you're not aware of it?'

Clare read and was startled by the message in his eyes. She had been just someone to put to good use so far, she had thought. Now he was looking at her and really seeing her.

'Men!' she said crossly, and began walking again, while he gave a little chuckle and followed her.

'So what's going to happen?' she asked as they reached the road. 'Do we leave, or what?'

Adam looked at her as though she were mad. 'Most certainly not! I shall work on Marcella. She was half-way inclined to do what I wanted once. She'll feel that way again.'

'Even if her better judgement tells her no?'

'She was interested enough to take the initiative in the first place. I think I'm capable of talking her round to that state of mind again.'

Clare condemned him with her clear grey eyes. 'Is there nothing you wouldn't do for the sake of your precious work?'

He outstared her. 'Nothing much.' They were back at the house. 'Let's get down to food,' he said, holding the door open for her to pass through, and then adding, the observation seeming strangely connected with their exchange, 'And where's the ring I provided? It should be on your finger.'

In the middle of the night Clare found herself sitting bolt upright in bed, the darkness around her still peopled with shapes from the nightmare that had driven her, choking and shouting, out of sleep and into an awakening no less horrible.

One shape looming out of the palpitating darkness was stronger and more threatening than the rest of the products of her terrified imagination, and she beat against the air, repeating, 'No! No!' with heightened intensity as she felt solid flesh against her fists.

'Clare, you're dreaming. It's all right, I'm putting on the light.'

The lamp on the little white-skirted table beside her bed cast a pool of light on the quilt, banishing the creatures of her mind and showing her Adam, barefoot in a black towelling robe, leaning over her.

Clare hugged her knees and rested her forehead on them, trying to calm her breathing and allow her heartbeat to slow down while she hid her face from him.

'What was it?' His hand touched her bare shoulder, warm and real, his voice concerned.

'The—' She shuddered. 'That awful place! Those people—Oh, lord!' She shook uncontrollably again at the memory of the catacombs which she had driven firmly to the depths of her mind since that afternoon, but which had surfaced maliciously in the unguarded hours of the night.

Adam swore softly and savagely. 'I could kill myself for that.' His grip tightened painfully on her flesh. 'Believe me, Clare, I had no idea that it would upset you so much, insensitive fool that I am.'

In her emotional state, his own self-reproach was painful to her.

'No——' she said, looking up at him, white-faced and trembling still, 'it wasn't just that. You didn't know—how could you? I let you think otherwise——' The words were coming fast now, the dam of grief breaking and letting her sorrow flood out. 'My mother didn't get better. She died.' It was said, and the relief of it brought tears pouring from Clare's eyes, the first tears, real tears, she had shed. 'Five weeks ago. I loved her very much. I—I——' She couldn't speak for the unuttered sobs blocking her throat, but she didn't need to say any more.

Adam sat on the side of the bed and pulled her into his arms, cuddling her against his chest and murmuring into her hair,

'You poor kid . . . Oh, you poor kid! And I sent you . . . That's it. Let yourself cry.'

She needed no encouragement now. With the word 'kid' ringing in her ears, she allowed herself to be held like a child while she sobbed, convulsively gripping him round his neck, not caring what she was doing, just responding to his kindness. She was not alone with her grief now as she had been over the past weeks. She was sharing it with someone. Oh, her father had been sad, she knew, but he had been able to put grief in its place, which, for him, was somewhere behind the arrangements to be made, the business to be run, the 'face' to be maintained at all costs. And Clare had, out of loyalty, gone along with his unspoken wishes for no fuss, but at a cost that she was only now beginning to realise.

Adam didn't say anything more. He just went on holding her, stroking her hair, letting her cry herself out until she came to a quivering halt, and, heedless of her appearance, raised a blotchy, swollen face from his chest.

'I'll get you a drink,' he said, gently releasing her at last. 'All right for a moment?'

'Mmm . . .' Clare said doubtfully. 'Something cold, please.'

'I shan't be long.'

She got out of bed while he was gone to find herself a dry handkerchief. With the drained, precarious calmness she was now feeling came self-awareness, and, catching sight of herself in the dressing-table mirror, she put off the bedside lamp and left just the kinder, more remote light shining across from Adam's room.

When he came back she took the milk he offered and drained it in one go, choking as the kick it contained—which owed nothing to the cow—hit her.

'What on earth did you put in it?' she croaked.

'Brandy—I thought you needed it. Better?'

She nodded. 'Thank you. Thank you for everything—not just the drink. I . . . I think I needed to do that. Cry, I mean. I'm sorry you happened to be around to put up with it.'

Adam ran his fingers through her hair. 'The least I could do was lend you a shoulder, in view of my own function as a trigger-mechanism for that outburst.' His hand trailed gently down her cheek, cupping her chin, making her look up at him. 'And you mustn't regret it in the least. Someone worth loving is worth crying over . . .'

When he took his hand away, Clare looked down, then blew her nose, not quite trusting herself to speak yet on that subject.

'Going to get to sleep again, do you think?' he asked.

'I expect so.' But she shivered as she slid down under the quilt again. 'I hope I don't get a repetition of that particular nightmare.'

'You won't, not now.' He sounded sure, but she was still a little afraid.

'What time is it?' she asked.

Adam turned his wrist to let the light from across the landing fall on his watch. 'Two o'clock.'

'A long time to morning . . .'

He hesitated, looking down at her, and Clare put out a hand in appeal, the brandy giving her courage to say what she knew she wanted.

'Could you—would you mind staying just a little bit—until I feel drowsy again?'

He took her hand firmly in his and pulled a chair over so that he could sit by the bed. 'This do?' Her hand was safe and warm in his, and she turned on her side so that she was facing his comfortingly large, shadowy shape. How could she have woven him into her nightmare figures? she asked herself bemusedly.

'Mmm . . . lovely,' she murmured into the pillow, drowsy already. For a while she floated in and out of sleep, comforted always by his silent presence and by the warm, loose clasp of his fingers round hers.

She must have slept for a while, because when she next briefly awoke there were bands of pale light between the slats of the shutters. Adam was still there, his eyes closed, so still that she didn't dare move herself, and soon she slept again.

It was bright daylight when she next awoke. Adam had gone, and she could hear sounds of vigorous splashing from the bathroom. Clare got up and closed her door, then flung open the shutters to lean out and look at the sparkling vista of the bay, spread out in fluid patches of purple and blue and peacock green. Strange rock towers crowned with cacti were catching the morning light just off shore.

What would it be like seeing Adam again after the uninhibited self-revelation she had gone in for under cover of darkness? Clare wondered. They had been two real people together for a little time, and it had been just what she needed at that point.

But how would it be from now on? Had they moved on to a different plane in their relationship—which so far had not been a relationship at all—and did she really want that to happen? It could complicate things. As long as they were in a state of reasonably impersonal mutual usefulness, it wasn't difficult for them to share a house. But if a more personal note crept into things . . .?

She heard Adam go downstairs, and, pulling off her nightdress, stepped under the shower.

I shall just have to go down and see how the land lies, she told herself, turning her face up to the water, and hoping that the said land would not prove to have been too extensively mined between last night and now.

CHAPTER FIVE

HAVING keyed herself up for some significant change in Adam's attitude towards her, and having even worked out the most diplomatic way of pointing out that she had not been quite herself in the small hours, for which she apologised, etcetera, Clare found it rather disconcerting that she hardly rated a glance when she walked into the kitchen.

'I'm going over to Marcella's,' said Adam. 'Coffee's made. Whatever else you want is up to you.' He was draining the last of his own coffee, his back towards her as he stood at the sink.

'I'll drive you over,' she volunteered quickly, wondering if there were a veiled reproach in his words for the fact that she was second down.

'Not necessary. And you haven't had your breakfast.'

'That doesn't matter. I don't always bother with any.'

He looked at her then. 'There's no need to make a martyr of yourself. Don't worry, when I want your services I'll make sure in advance that I get them. This morning I intend walking over to the *palazzo* and back.'

Clare felt a slight sinking of disappointment. She hadn't wanted too much of a change in his attitude after last night, but he was being so brisk and detached that she felt he could have gone less far in that particular direction.

'Then at least leave me the washing-up to do,' she

pleaded lamely.

'Don't fuss! There are some books in my room. Take one out to the garden or something with my blessing. I don't want to have to concern myself with how you're going to occupy your time.'

He was only half thinking of what he was saying, she could tell, now that he had turned round and was facing her. His eyes had the preoccupied, intense look she was beginning to realise was associated with the ticking over of the Melvin business brain. Perversely, now that he had so clearly shown that the happenings of the night and their emotions were strictly transitory, she had a driving need to remind him of them. She really couldn't understand herself.

'Adam——' He stopped over by the door.

'Yes?'

'I'm sorry about last night. Thank you for being so kind to me.'

'No problem,' he said carelessly. 'My brother was prone to nightmares. It's second nature to me to act as anchor-man against the bogeys.'

It wasn't like that, Clare wanted to protest . . . not entirely. It was real sadness, not imaginary, that you helped me to cope with. But Adam had obviously finished with the subject and she felt snubbed for having mentioned it. Serve me right, she thought.

'I didn't know you had a brother,' she said, snatching at the chance to change the subject.

'I don't suppose you did. An exchange of family backgrounds hasn't got much to do with what we're here for, after all, has it?'

If that wasn't a slap in the face for her because of last night, then she was more of a fool than she already felt herself to be. Clare began hacking away at yesterday's loaf, glad to hide behind the forward swing of her damp hair. She needn't have bothered. Adam was rolling down the sleeves of his dark blue shirt and shrugging on the jacket of his pale grey suit, already more with Marcella than here in the kitchen with her.

'Amuse yourself, if you can. There's money on the table if you need it,' he said briefly, then the door closed and Clare was alone.

She swallowed a stupid lump that had appeared from nowhere and lodged in her throat. He had been so nice last night, she thought a touch tearfully. People shouldn't treat you as if you mattered one minute and then were a great big nuisance the next.

The irony of her thoughts struck her. What sort of switch in her own attitude was that? You're crazy, she chided herself. Get busy and stop the self-pitying brooding.

Breakfast and the small amount of kitchen tidying necessary took only a small slice of the morning. Clare decided to go and get some fresh bread in case Adam wanted to eat a snack lunch. Knowing what he had in mind for the rest of the day would have helped, she thought with a last vestige of pique as she threw the remains of yesterday's bread to the gulls from the garden wall.

She negotiated her purchase at the baker's quite successfully by means of gestures and blind faith that the price she was charged and the change she was given were correct. The 'thank you' exchange she learned from the two women ahead of her in the shop, practising them silently to herself . . . *Grazie* . . . *Prego* . . . But when the woman behind the counter fired a rapid question at her, Clare had to shrug hopelessly to indicate her lack of understanding.

There was more to San Paolo than she had realised. Narrow streets formed quite a maze beyond the square. Sounds of children from high, open windows indicated the school, and the fort-like building discharging a cluster of elderly women down its steps was obviously the church. The café tables were empty this morning, so no cries of '*Bona*!' followed her progress across the square.

Once she had deposited the bread, she explored a little further beyond the house and saw that there was a path down as well as up, so it was possible to get to the beach provided one had the agility of a goat. This morning when she had looked down there had been quite a strip of silvery sand. It was good to think she could take advantage of it when the slight movement of the tide allowed.

Clare sat on a rock for a while, absorbing the air heavy with the scent of thyme and mint. She could hear cattle bells coming from much further back along the headland. An electric-green lizard ran swiftly out from the shelter of a stone and froze, motionless, to warm up in the sun.

She went back to the house and involved herself in another flurry of activity, cleaning the bathroom and her own shower-room, then, after studying the food cupboard, making a salade Niçoise for lunch.

She was just putting it in the fridge when Adam erupted—there was no other word for it—into the house, far sooner than Clare had anticipated in view of the fact that he had walked both ways.

'You've been very quick,' she said, sensing trouble.

'A masterpiece of the obvious, as statements go.' He threw his jacket on the nearest chair and began flinging cupboard doors open. 'Isn't there anything to drink in this damned place?'

She silently held out a glass of lemonade, adding a deprecating, 'At least it's cool,' as he took it and tossed it back. 'Dare I ask how you got on?' she ventured.

'I didn't get on at all. Chance would have been a fine thing. I walked there and I walked back—that about sums it up. The woman's taken her hook. Gone off on urgent business, according to the maid who answered the door. Madam goes away often. No message for the *Signor. Scusi, scusi, scusi*!' Adam's voice rose as he mimicked the servant.

'What are you going to do, then?' Clare bit her lip as she realised that the question had pleased him little the last time she had put it to him, and it was likely to please him even less now.

'I'd like to be in a position to answer that.' He was striding to and fro like a caged tiger, thinking aloud. 'If she'd only stayed around, I know I could have persuaded her—I just know it. But now that she's packed up and run, I'm stymied. I could probably find out where she's gone, but she's made her meaning so plain that there's damn all to gain from following her around.'

'You don't know when she's likely to be back?'

'Either she didn't say or I wasn't being told. Your guess is as good as mine. The most I could do was slip the gardener a fistful of lire to let me know if and when she turns up again. There was no joy to be had from the maid.' He drove one clenched hand into the palm of the other. 'What a bloody waste of time! What a futile load of hanging around we're in for now!'

'It's a lovely place to hang around in.' Clare's attempt at a Pollyanna job failed dismally. Adam gave her a withering look which indicated that he didn't think the remark merited an answer.

'I've made us some lunch,' she said, trying again.

'It's not food I'm wanting.' He hovered in the doorway, frustrated plans having taken all purpose out of his day, then he shrugged and raised his hands in capitulation. 'All right, get the food out while I go and change. Then the minute we've eaten you can drive me into Castellammare and we'll stock up.'

Mainly on liquid commodities, I bet! Clare thought while he was upstairs. A fine time of it they'd have if Adam Melvin intended drinking his way through the next few days! However, she would have to cope with the situation . . . and it was only for two weeks. It's no good keeping on saying that, she told herself ruefully. A lot can happen in two weeks. A lot's happened already . . .

She was right about the nature of the shopping. They got a certain amount of food—things they could keep in the freezer to use when they didn't feel like going out, Adam said in one of their brief spoken exchanges, looking as though as far as he was concerned he wasn't remotely interested in going anywhere. The bulk of the shopping, though, was of the kind that came in bottles and clinked noisily in the bags.

Adam started on the whisky as soon as they were back, telling Clare to help herself to what she wanted.

'No, thank you,' she told him quietly.

'The sun not far enough over the yardarm for you?' he queried as he spread his books and papers over the table.

'I don't happen to like whisky, and I don't want a drink now, that's all,' she answered quickly. If he suspected she was being self-righteous he was wrong. But she was feeling disappointed. Resorting to drink was the action of a weak man, and she had thought Adam strong. She hated to see him so upset by a mere hiccup in his work schedule.

She looked round the immaculate house. Nothing to do there for the moment.

'Do you want me for a while?' she asked.

He didn't look up. 'No, do what you like.' He was staring intently at a map of Sicily.

'Then it's all right if I go down to the beach?'

The dark blue eyes glanced briefly in her direction. 'My dear Clare, it's all right if you go to the moon for the next couple of hours as far as I'm concerned. Is that clear enough for you?'

'Is the sea safe for swimming here? Sorry, but I have to know.'

'The Mediterranean doesn't exactly go in for tide races,' he said with pitying patience.

'And may I get one of your books?'

'Didn't I tell you you could, earlier on?' It was obvious that his patience was running out—fast.

'Thank you,' said Clare with determined politeness, resolved to keep up the civilities no matter how little time he had for them.

She ran upstairs and selected a couple of paperbacks—a Penguin anthology of short stories, and a psychological whodunnit. Then she changed into her turquoise bikini and collected a towel, sun-lotion and glasses, managing to leave the house without encountering Adam again.

She was boiling hot when she eventually reached the strip of sand that the slight movement of the sea had once again revealed. Dropping her things, she ran thankfully into the water and swam almost to the end of the headland, then a little way out so that she could get a good view of the house in its rocky eyrie. It was an extraordinary place to build, but incredibly beautiful.

She swam slowly back to the strip of sand again and spread out her towel after drying herself. Now for a lazy hour's sunbathing, after which she would steel herself to go up and face whatever state Adam was in.

She read a chapter or two of the whodunnit, but it didn't seem the day for dark deeds and villainy. After a while she put it down and turned to the short stories. There was an inscription on the title page, she noticed as she looked for the list of contents. Bold, artistic writing . . . 'Happy birthday, darling. Fay.' Clare was about to turn hurriedly over, feeling that the mere fact of her eyes resting on the words written by Adam's wife was an unforgivable intrusion, when she saw the date. The year was three years previous to the current one—but the day and the month were the same. Today's date. Today was Adam's birthday.

She sat and digested the fact. Maybe this was the thing that accounted for his mood. Perhaps special days like birthdays were occasions when you missed people you had loved all the more intensely. Blunting his mind with whisky suddenly seemed more understandable, more pardonable. Poor Adam, he must have loved his wife so much . . . After last night she knew what warmth, what softness there was in him. She had experienced it herself.

For a while she dwelt on the feel of his arms round her, his steady, patient waiting for her to cry herself out, and the hours he had just sat there in the darkness, letting reassurance flow from his fingers to hers while she slept. She owed him for that.

She resolved not to let his birthday pass in misery if she could help it. She would make a special meal—do her level best to make him forget his unhappiness a little. The village could come up with something in the way of fresh food, she was sure, and if she had to use Adam's own money to get it—well, he could deduct it from her wages.

Full of determination, she picked up her things and toiled up the path again. Adam had disappeared—out into the garden, she saw when she had a discreet peep out of the window. The whisky bottle too—but not too much had gone from it. Maybe he was feeling a bit better already, and she would soon deal with any remaining gloom.

Clare dressed quickly and hunted around until she found table mats and pretty glasses. There was a treasure trove of brightly coloured napkins and a box of candles at the back of one of the drawers. The cutlery would have to wait until she knew what they would be eating, and the flowers she would sneak from the garden at the last minute, and hope that Adam wouldn't notice.

A surprise stroke of luck and happy timing made her reach the square just as one of the local fishermen was setting out a makeshift display of his catch. Nothing that she fancied for a main course, but there were oysters. Six for Adam, four for herself—that would make a special starter. Rotten luck if he didn't like them, but she would risk if for the sake of the distinction it would give the opening of the meal.

The general store proved to be a surprising goldmine. There was superb-looking steak in the cold counter. Steak au poivre, salad and new potatoes, Clare decided. There were fresh raspberries too. She bought lots of them, and by dint of pouring gestures over them managed to convey 'cream' to the shopkeeper, who triumphantly produced it.

Clare hurried back. By six-thirty everything was ready. A bowl of flowers which she had managed to get surreptitiously from the bed nearest the house was scenting the room, appetising smells were wafting from the kitchen, and the candles were lit.

Clare went into the garden and called, 'Dinner's ready!' then scuttled excitedly back into the house to await Adam's reaction.

She saw him stretch his arms widely, then get up and walk towards the house, rubbing the back of his neck. She stood by the table, her face eager with anticipation.

He came in, paused as the spectacle in all its glory registered, then looked expressionlessly at her.

'What's all this in aid of?'

Clare beamed and said triumphantly, 'To wish you a happy birthday!'

His expression still did not change. 'How did you find that out?'

'From the book of yours I borrowed.'

He pulled out his chair and slumped into it. 'Pity you didn't choose another one,' he said shortly.

Clare's pleasure was seeping slowly out of her, being replaced by the feeling that she had gone somehow appallingly wrong.

'I—I just thought it would be——'

'Sit down,' he interrupted, his voice thick with tiredness. 'I know what you thought. What you didn't know is that I was unwise enough to marry on my birthday. Today also happens to be my wedding anniversary.'

Clare felt physically winded by the shock of his words. Her heart hit rock bottom with a dreadful jolt.

'—And in the circumstances, the least useful thing I could be offered as a starter is a damned aphrodisiac,' he went on, thrusting away the oysters on their bed of leaves.

Clare couldn't speak. She reached out blindly and snuffed the candles with her bare fingers, feeling nothing. Somehow she managed to choke out, 'I'm so sorry, Adam,' before fleeing to the kitchen with the plates of oysters.

Once they were disposed of, she stood there not knowing what to do, feeling dreadful. Eventually Adam called out,

'Well, come on, bring in the next thing. Don't hang about out there!' He appeared in the doorway, looking not angry, just terribly depressed and trying to hide it. 'The best thing we can do,' he said, not unkindly, 'is go back to square one and pretend that that little scene didn't happen. This is a day like any other. You've cooked a meal. Let's eat it.'

They did—but it was more like a wake than the celebration Clare had planned, and she did more pushing of food round her plate than actually eating. It was a relief when Adam pushed his chair back in sudden decision and said explosively,

'Let's get out of this place. I need a mountain-top to blow my thoughts away!'

She was on her feet before he had finished speaking.

Erice, where he directed her to drive, appeared at first as a distant crest of castle towers on the mountain they were approaching. The road switchbacked and zigzagged through pine forests carpeted with borage and calendula, and blazing here and there with fuchsias and flowering Judas trees. When the trees gave way from time to time like curtains parting, the view over the sea was spectacular.

They reached the top of the town itself, and parked, walking through the quiet streets, unashamedly spying on the quiet courtyards. Grey walls in the narrow streets spilled over with mantles of ivy and were crowned with pots of bright flowers. Arched gateways revealed a moving picture of family life. Among the houses were crumbling mini-palaces with baroque facades, flights of stone steps hollowed out by centures of passing feet—and over all an air of calm peace that worked into the heart, stilling the disturbed feelings of the earlier evening.

Adam disappeared into a pastry shop just off the cobbled main square and came out with almond cakes, a speciality of the town. They ate them leaning on the wall at the end of the piazza, looking down the dramatic two-thousand-foot drop where the mountainside flaunted skirts of blue borage, yellow mayflowers and purple vetch on to the plain of Trapani below. The silence between them had been transformed from the strained to the companionable, Clare thought thankfully as she gazed over the golden sea on which floated misty visions of land.

'The nearest land you can see is the Engadi Islands,' Adam told her. 'And that blur on the horizon is the coast of Africa—not often you can see that, it's usually too hazy. Must be a special show put on for your benefit.

Clare looked up at him and smiled, and he reached out and squeezed her hand as it rested on the wall as though to reassure her that all was well between them. She felt a great contentment. The breeze was blowing through her thoughts, as Adam had said it would, and sending her hair flying out from her head like a silken banner. The unbelievable scents of the flowers and herbs below them were borne up in heady profusion. It was a moment to treasure.

'What's the history of this town?' she asked curiously. So many fingers from the past seemed to reach out to her from the ancient stones.

'Hard to separate it from legend. It's the site of a very old temple of Venus, for one thing. And do you remember Daedalus? The one who—'

Clare made flapping movements with her arms and he nodded. 'Yes—he flew from Crete with his son on wings of wax and feathers to escape Minos's disfavour.'

'And Icarus flew too near the sun and it melted the wax so that he fell into the sea and was drowned . . .' said Clare, feeling suddenly that it could all be true, not legend. Up here one could be intoxicated into thinking natural flight humanly possible.

'Yes. Well, Daedalus is said to have created a golden honeycomb so real that even the bees were fooled by it, as an offering to Venus. Men have searched for it for centuries, with no luck. But the legend I like best is about the release of white doves from the mountain top at the end of winter. Nine days later they fly back, led by a red dove—she symbolises Astarte, the goddess of fertility, and the return of spring.'

'I can picture them.' Clare leaned out from the

wall, her imagination filling the sky with white and scarlet wings beating against the setting sun. 'I love all this talk of gods and goddesses. Which shall we be, Adam?'

His dark eyes assessed her, lingering on the soft, honey-coloured skin, the shining hair already streaked with gold from the day's sun, the eager grey eyes, the blue silk of her dress where the breeze pressed it lovingly against the curves beneath it.

'I think Astarte for you,' he said, something in his look and the tone of his voice making her heart gallop and her eyes drop down from his. Then he pricked the bubble of the moment with his next words. 'I, of course, as I'm sure you've already decided, am a prime candidate for Bacchus. Come on, nymph, we'd better get back. Once night starts to fall, it falls quickly, and you know what the road's like.'

He found a Beethoven quartet on the car radio as they drove back to San Paolo, and there was no further talking—but the return was a different matter from the setting out.

They dumped the dinner dishes in the sink to be dealt with next morning, then Adam said with gentle dismissiveness, 'I expect you're tired now. I'm going to listen to the World Service news before I come up.'

Clare hovered for a moment, wanting to say something but not sure what. In the end she compromised with her thoughts.

'I loved Erice. Thank you for showing it to me.' What she really meant was, I loved the way you were in Erice. Thank you for being like that. She wanted to say that she hoped the day hadn't been too painful for him. That the beauty of the world seen from their mountain-top and even the fact that she had been there with him had done something to make him feel better. She thought it all, and said none of it.

Adam was running through the jumbled voices on the airwaves, only half an ear directed towards her.

'Yes . . . good place,' he said absentmindedly. 'Ah, here we are.' Cultured English tones delivered the facts about less pleasant things going on in the world.

'Well, goodnight, then.' Clare wasn't even sure that he heard her at all.

She was tired and she fell asleep quickly, but some time later a sudden noise awakened her abruptly, followed by another dull thud.

She listened for a moment, then cautiously switched on her lamp to check the time. Three o'clock. She wondered apprehensively about intruders and crept across to open her door and rouse Adam, but the landing light was on, Adam's bedroom door open, and his bed undisturbed. So he was the most likely maker of the noise. Clare debated the wisdom of going down to ask if he was all right. If he had chosen to stay up so late, he probably had been wanting his own company and wouldn't take kindly to her intrusion. But there had been those bumps . . . Suppose he had had an accident? That thought decided her. She grabbed her silk kimono and flew downstairs, tying it as she went.

Adam was sprawled in one of the comfortable chairs, fast asleep. It was not hard to see why. There was a glass and the whisky bottle beside him. There were three or four scattered books, their pages bent double in the slide from his lap, on the floor beside him, and they obviously had caused the noise that roused her.

Clare picked them up carefully and put them on the table, her eyes on Adam's face. She couldn't very well leave him there. He'd wake up in the morning all stiff and aching—and incredibly bad-tempered. Gently she put a hand on his shoulder.

'Adam? Adam?'

The thick dark lashes flickered and slowly his eyes opened. For a moment he stared at her, confused, then a glimmer of amusement stirred.

'The lovely Astarte, no less.' His voice was sufficiently blurred to make Clare realise that she should be wary.

'Not at all—only me. You've fallen asleep down here and it's very late,' she said calmly.

He stretched. 'Who's for bed, then?' One arm reached out with sudden speed, caught her off balance as she leaned over him, and pulled her on to his knee.

'That's more like it,' he said. 'Nice, very nice. Goddesses are all very well, but a warm, human woman is definitely better.' He pulled her head into the hollow of his neck, sighing contentedly, and his chin pinned her firmly and not too comfortably in place.

'Adam, this is silly!' Clare protested, her voice muffled against the tickly stretch of bare chest in his open shirt neck. She was hanging on to reason and dignity, but not exactly winning. One of his arms was holding her firmly against him, the other hand was wandering hypnotically to and fro over the shiny tautness of her kimono where it was pulled tight across her thighs, doing things to her will-power it wouldn't do to dwell upon.

'Silky . . .' Adam said thoughtfully, 'Like your hair.' His hand moved upwards, sliding voluptuously slowly until his fingers reached her hair and twisted the smooth rope of it round his palm.

'You don't know what you're doing!' gasped Clare, knowing that she should be moving away, but her body seemed to have rebelled against her mind and it was refusing to obey her.

'Don't I?' Adam tugged gently so that her face was turned up to his. 'I've had the desire to do this ever since I watched you leaning on that wall in Erice, gazing out at flights of mythical doves . . .'

His mouth touched hers, and Clare stiffened in resistance, then, as his gentle authority overcame her tension, her lips parted with the inevitability of a flower obeying the warm, insistent command of the sun. She felt dizzy with the yearning sweetness that possessed her, and she knew in that instant that if this miracle of feeling came from a kiss, then she had never been truly kissed before.

She came out of her trance to find his eyes glittering down into hers while she gazed at him, the whole of her soul exposed and vulnerable, it seemed.

' "Sweet Clare, make me immortal with a kiss," ' he said softly, laughter lurking in his voice.

He was teasing her. He could make her succumb to this dangerous, this mind-blowing hurricane of feeling—and he could laugh at her like this.

'Wrong woman, Adam,' she said, trying to make her voice sound casually amused too. 'That was Helen of Troy, and the words were Marlowe's, not yours.'

'But the feeling behind them is universal.' The deep huskiness of his voice, whether sincere or mocking, reached a spot deep inside her and threatened to reduce her to weak compliance again.

'Stop it, Adam!' With a surge of strength she broke away from him and stood up, breathing fast.

'"Had we but world enough and time, This coyness, lady, were no crime . . ." ' he went on quoting at her, changing poets but sticking to his theme.

'Get up and come to bed,' ordered Clare. 'All this is whisky talking.'

'I thought it was Andrew Marvell, but if that was a genuine invitation . . .' His wicked satyr's grin accompanied the words.

'Your *own* bed,' she said doggedly.

'You disappoint me. You really do.' He sighed over-dramatically, then stood up. She suddenly found her waist squeezed in a firm grip.

'At least we can go upstairs like friends,' he said contentedly.

Friends! Marvell's words echoed in Clare's mind and bedevilled her senses as they climbed the stairs. She had no way of knowing for certain if Adam needed her help or not, but she gave him the benefit of the doubt since he was acting so much out of character, and, once in his bedroom, stooped to slip off his shoes.

'I don't go in for pyjamas,' he said innocently.

Like hell he was innocent! 'That,' she said firmly, 'is your problem, not mine. You can sleep in your clothes.' She stood and turned smartly, but not quickly enough. Adam was holding the back of her kimono in a vice-like grip.

When she half turned, he was glinting up at her

through half-closed eyes.

'You haven't kissed me goodnight.'

'Let go, Adam,' she said with pained patience.

'Just a little birthday kiss,' he persisted. 'Every guy gets a kiss on his birthday, for goodness' sake.'

She waited a moment, then stooped towards him, since it seemed the only thing to do if she was to get away. She meant it to be a hurried peck on his forehead, but he was too quick for her, and too schemingly clever. He moved his head so that once again his lips could take possession of hers.

Even if she had tried to pull away, she couldn't have done so, because his hands were gripping her shoulders now. But again, a feeling so strong went through Clare's body, dissolving her will, insidiously undermining her physical strength, that it left her staring breathlessly down at Adam, whose shadowy face looked up into hers with the same still intensity.

He gave a long, contented sigh and closed his eyes.

'Not too bad a day, little Clare. Better for having you around.' He was still hanging on to her hand. 'Sit here a bit longer. Just a bit. A reciprocal,' he stumbled slightly over the word, 'a reciprocal gesture, if you like.'

Still under the spell of his kiss, Clare sank down on to the edge of the bed, staring at their linked hands. It was getting to be a habit, this hand-holding. First her room last night, now this. But last night had been different. There had been no vibrant sense of something strange and miraculous about to happen, as she had felt so unmistakably tonight.

She looked down on Adam's face as it slowly relaxed into sleep. A bitter-sweet tenderness coursed through her, confusing and yet promising at the same time.

What was happening to her? She tried to rationalise the sequence of events. Adam was unhappy, so he had had too much to drink. He had behaved—because of that simple fact—as he never would in normal circumstances. So much was easy.

But what of herself? Honesty compelled her to go on. She had no such excuse, no such easy explanation for the way she had felt twice . . . for the way she was feeling now as she looked down on his sleeping face.

She was crazy. She had to be crazy to let a man's easily aroused passion drug her into thinking there was something special about the way he had apparently enjoyed kissing her.

Adam stirred and murmured something unintelligible in his sleep. Unintelligible until the last word, which stood out clearly—Fay.

Clare felt it like a slap in the face, like a bucket of cold water thrown over her to bring her back to her senses. Adam was frowning now, his face drawn as though his dream tormented him.

He had not, in reality, been kissing her at all, she thought with painful humiliation. He had been thinking of his lost wife and his lost happiness. Even now, while she sat here dreaming and obediently holding his hand, he was caught up in an illusion of past happiness and pain, drawing no comfort from the warm actuality of her own touch.

Gently she loosened his fingers and slipped her hand out of his, pity for his unconscious self-betrayal overcoming her own feelings.

Poor, sad Adam . . .

The last lines of Andrew Marvell's poignantly

erotic poem to his coy mistress imprinted themselves on Clare's mind and made her shiver with the coldness of reality as she trod softly back to her own room.

> The grave's a fine and private place,
> But none, I think, do there embrace.

He had been right, that long-dead poet. It all ended in nothing.

CHAPTER SIX

'COME ON! Get your cases packed!'

Clare awoke to pounding on her bedroom door and Adam's cheerful order. She got out of bed and went over to look blearily out of her room on to the landing.

'What's going on?' she asked. 'Are we going home?'

'Is that your only suggestion? It seems to crop up every other minute.' Adam was already dressed and looked as fresh as the day in his white jeans and grey and white check shirt. 'No, not home,' he went on. 'I've decided that since we're supposed to be holidaymakers, and since—damn it!—we're not fortunate enough to have anything more urgent to do at the moment, we're going to wander round and have ourselves a holiday. Erice went down well last night, so why not the rest of Sicily?'

Clare eyed him cautiously. 'Oh. You remember Erice, do you?'

'Why shouldn't I?' He looked blandly back at her, his expression so politely enquiring that she wondered if she had dreamed up the happenings of last night. If so, she had a strange capacity for torturing herself into wakefulness, because awake she had certainly been for quite a time after she had left Adam and gone back to her own room. And yet this morning he looked perfectly normal and quite unabashed by what had happened.

'Forget it,' she said. 'I'm still half asleep. I didn't

mean anything.'

'A very dangerous place, half-way between sleeping and waking. Anything can happen.' He ruffled her hair cheekily and made off downstairs, leaving her to wonder even more just how much of last night was clear in his mind. He obviously didn't intend giving anything away.

Clare stood there indecisively for a moment, then she shrugged and pulled her case out from under the bed. Adam was the boss. If he said "Go", they went. She yawned hugely. She certainly had to hand it to him for stamina! She forced her thoughts away from last night and began to pack.

A strange, unreal, wonderful time followed—a time of sunkissed, magic days when it was easy for Clare to forget the reason that had brought them to Sicily. It seemed as though she had always known Adam, as they wandered through towns and villages as old as time, sprawled companionably on quiet beaches away from the tourist areas and absorbed the sights and sounds of the island. Adam seemed totally relaxed, the tension and purposefulness of the early days put aside and replaced by a warm, easy charm.

Their conversations were fleshing him out for her, except in the one unbroached area of his marriage. She learned that his parents ran a bookshop in Norfolk, and that his brother Chris still took advantage of the comfortable family home in vacations from Manchester University where he had just completed a degree course which had so far not pointed in any career direction. Adam spoke of his brother with affectionate indulgence. Chris, he told her, was taking a year off now to 'bum around Europe', as he put it. Clare found it intriguingly strange that Adam should speak of this almost with envy. He had seemed so work-orientated . . . though now he seemed totally immersed in enjoyment of their wanderings.

Sometimes, after a period of quietness, Adam would begin to say something—on a topic completely unrelated to what they were doing or had been previously discussing—and Clare would find with a shock that his words and her unspoken thoughts matched uncannily. Some intangible link seemed to be growing between them, a bond that alternately comforted and frightened her. Because it couldn't last. This . . . friendship, for want of a better word—a word that she could face up to—was born of the present circumstances, and all too soon the magic would end.

She told herself it was the sense of time reaching back all around them that added depth and strength to what was perhaps just compatibility. Adam was good to be with, that was the simple truth of it. He was stimulating company, and he knew so much about the places they saw. His curiosity about the things that were new to him was infectious, and being with someone who reacted with Adam's sensitivity to the beauty of the places and architecture they found on their enchanted journey enhanced what couldn't help but be a wonderful experience.

Thus Clare reasoned with herself, but insidiously the silken threads tightened around her heart.

Once, in a crowded city street, she saw someone who reminded her suddenly of Giles—almost the first time she had thought of him, she realised with a shock, since she left England. How unreal he seemed now . . . a ghost figure from a past that was unsubstantial, totally lacking in colour beside the vibrant present.

The knowledge that all too soon it must end rebounded on her, bringing with it so strong a sense of grief that Clare examined her feelings more seriously. She wondered if she could possibly be doing something so unwise as to fall in love with Adam, but always there was something to see, something urgent to do, so that she could push the thought to the back of her mind.

It wasn't until they reached Taormina on the east coast, where they were to stay for a couple of days, that the thought took root and refused to be dismissed . . . became a growing certainty that made Clare both melt with happiness and freeze with dread that she would one day soon inevitably find herself cast out from her fool's paradise.

They had arrived in Taormina early in the afternoon, moving on from the hot, dusty interior, and Adam had found a suite for them in a hotel looking towards the mountains in the north, and, from a side window, across the sea to the coast and hills of Calabria.

They wandered through the little town, pleasant with its main street closed to traffic. By a happy chance a touring ballet company from France was performing *Swan Lake* in the open-air Greek theatre that night, and by an even happier chance two tickets had been returned to the box office just before Adam defied the 'Sold Out' stickers across the posters and called in to enquire.

'It's an experience not to be missed,' he told Clare. 'You'll know why when you see the theatre.'

Over dinner Clare was quiet, and he asked if she was tired.

'No!' she said, surfacing guiltily from thoughts that she must at all costs hide from him. 'I'm just full of good food and so many lovely things we've seen today.'

'Good—because I want us to walk to the theatre—more for the return journey than anything else. Taormina's little streets by night are something special.'

As they walked along the Via Teatro Greco in the tidal wave of theatre-going people, Clare was aware that she was attracting admiring glances. There was nothing surreptitious about the men bestowing them. She put it down to the dress she was wearing—silk, the colour of pale flax, simple in colour, wickedly clinging in cut. Adam had looked at her reflectively when she came out of her room, and she had touched her hair, pinned up in an asymmetric topknot into which she had tucked a creamy rose filched from the arrangement in their suite.

'Have I overdone it?' she asked him nervously, her grey eyes huge as she questioned him.

He shook his head with a little smile. 'No. You've done the evening proud.'

What Clare didn't realise as they approached the ancient theatre was that the glow that aroused response in every man they passed owed nothing to the clothes and everything to the happiness that the time and the place and above all Adam's company created in her. She could have walked along beside him in rags, looking up at him as they talked, and still there would have been something about her to turn heads and bring smiles to faces.

'Oh!' Her gasp as they emerged into the bowl of the theatre was something she couldn't suppress.

The theatre itself, with its arches and columns and tiers of crumbling stone seats in the gaps and crannies of which tiny green-leaved plants ran riot, was spectacle enough, but the natural backcloth was out of this world. Beyond the columns rose green-topped hills, and beyond the hills, hanging like a mirage in the intense blue of the sky, was the snowy, dazzling crest of Mount Etna.

Clare sat spellbound, and when the music began and the petal-light dancers floated across the stage she was utterly entranced. Nothing could exceed the emotion aroused in her by this moment, she thought. Nothing in the world, surely.

But something could. Adam was taking her hand in his. She looked down at their joined hands, hers small and golden, almost hidden in his larger, darker grasp. Slowly she looked at him, unable to believe the aching, tremulous happiness that filled her, greater far than anything she had so far experienced.

He was looking down at her, then he leaned closer so that his words tickled her cheek as he said in the softest of whispers,

'Before you accuse me again, I know exactly what I'm doing. You look as though if I don't anchor you, you'll be floating away into some wonderland or other!'

Again, he had said, betraying himself with that one word. So he had remembered all that happened the night before they left San Paolo. He was even, obliquely, reminding her of it. And if he didn't mind about their shared remembering, could she dare let the tiny spark of hope that had pricked into life deep inside her lay its claim to a lasting, even a growing place? She looked sideways at Adam, but he was gazing intently at the stage and his profile betrayed nothing.

She had this moment, and this physical contact, though. Her fingers curled round his, and she thought she detected an answering pressure. As the ballet progressed, awareness of their linked hands added a new, voluptuous layer to the evening's pleasure.

They walked back to the hotel afterwards through a dark maze of narrow streets and stone steps heavy with the scent of flowers cascading over walls. The perfume was heady as wine, and stars seemed to dance overhead in the gaps between the rooftops.

It was a night loaded in favour of love, and Clare ached to succumb to its enchantment. Her feelings frightened her. She wanted with an urgency she had never known to spend the rest of the night in Adam's room, in his bed, in his arms.

He had ordered champagne to be waiting, chilled, for them, but when he took up the bottle to draw the cork he was talking about the performance as matter-of-factly as though they had never touched each other, and suddenly she could neither bear it nor trust herself in his presence a second longer. She pleaded tiredness when she should have pleaded love-madness, and shut herself in her room.

In her bed, she tried to calm down. She was suffering from holiday fever, she told herself. No one could fall in love as quickly as she had done—or imagined she had done. She had known Giles for a couple of years, and not a fraction of the turbulence Adam seemed to arouse in her had marked that relationship. She dredged up all the reasons why it couldn't be happening to her—rebound effects, freedom going to her head, reaction to the sadness she had experienced. She listened to herself, but she didn't believe a word of it. Her heart was telling her something different, and her heart seemed to have developed a strange, frightening power.

Next day they climbed the flights of stone steps linking the loops of the serpentine road up to the heights of Castel Mola. On the way they stopped to see the sanctuary of the Madonna della Rocca, bright with offerings of fresh flowers other pilgrims had brought.

'Let me come to my senses,' Clare prayed with sudden urgency, only to hear Adam ask as they climbed on,

'What was your particular need, then, Clare?'

'Strength to finish this climb,' she invented flippantly, and as they drank almond wine in the café and looked out over the terraced vines and groves of citrus fruits she forced herself to be bright and amusing so that he said, with the first trace of displeasure that she had seen in him for days,

'Seems that whoever heard that request of yours overdid the hand-out. You're entertaining the whole café!'

That night they went to their separate rooms early so that they could be up in time to make the three a.m. ascent of Etna, and as they drove through the darkness up to the Rifugio Sapienza where they were to get the cable car link and then the jeep to the crater, Clare managed to fool herself that she had indeed been a little crazy yesterday, drunk on music and beauty and the scent of flowers. Today she felt sane, concentrated, controlled again.

At the crater's edge, though, as she stood horrified but spellbound by the red, seething agitation of the glowing lava, the words of the guide, spoken in charming, accented English out of courtesy to them, seemed to have special significance. The molten core of the earth, capable of rising in savage fury to hurl rocks fifteen miles and more on to the city of Catania, seemed a frightening parallel to the feelings she was discovering in herself, feelings as far-reaching in their effect as the strength of the volcano. She would go home and leave Adam . . . but would she ever get away from him in her mind?

As they watched, discreetly left alone by the guide, for the land far below to emerge from the dark morning mists into the dawn they were privileged to see from this eyrie in the skies, Clare felt as though she were being shown the whole world at her feet, only to be reminded that it would be a terrifyingly empty place without Adam.

'What do you want from life, Clare?' he asked her suddenly, making her wonder if he could actually read her mind. 'Are you any closer to a proper decision about what you'll do—a more appropriate job?'

It was only a polite question. What would he do if she told him that there was nothing she would like more than to spend the rest of her life with him?

'That's a big question,' she said tamely.

'Then this is the place to answer it. They say that up here the air's so pure that it makes the mind act with incredible freedom. Come on, apply yourself to the question. Don't dodge it because it's a big one.'

'The honest answer is that I just don't know,' Clare said carefully. 'Several times I've thought I had everything pigeonholed, and it's turned out that I'd got it all wrong.' And that was before I met you, she thought with a pang.

'That's no reason to opt out of planning completely.'

'Maybe it is. Maybe if I sit back and just let things happen without definite ideas, something good will come out of it, like—' She had been going to say 'like coming to Sicily with you', but that, of course, could not be said. And maybe it wasn't at all good in the long run, anyway.

'Like what?' he prompted.

His insistence—or maybe it was the quality of the air that he had told her about—fused a recklessness in her. She was on top of the world—literally on top of the world. The man she loved—yes, here she could do nothing but admit it—was coming as close to the subject that ate away at her mind and heart as he ever would. Maybe this was the one moment that could be the dividing point in her life, sending her either on to happiness, or into a darkness she couldn't bear to contemplate. More fool she if she made no attempt to test the balance, to see if it could possibly swing in the direction she longed for it to go.

'Let's forget me and talk about you,' she said, her heartbeat quickening with her daring. 'Are you any closer to breaking away from the past?'

Now Adam was looking at her, his dark blue eyes alert, and for both of them the sunrise went on unheeded. His expression was unreadable, but at least she had his attention.

'And what do you mean by that?'

She swallowed hard. 'You know what I mean. One sad experience needn't spoil the rest of your life.'

His mouth hardened. 'What makes you think my life is spoiled? I have a job that I find extremely fulfilling. I have friends. I have experiences like the current one, which—up to now—has not been without enjoyment.'

Clare had to go on. 'You're avoiding the real question. If I have to spell it out, I will. If you won't let yourself be prepared to love anyone again, ever, what do you think will happen to you in the end? If you don't know, I'll tell you. You'll grow colder and colder. That lovely house of yours will echo around you. The dark corners will grow darker, the days will seem longer . . . How can you let that happen to yourself?'

Was this really herself, speaking so passionately? Clare thought wildly over the pounding of her heart.

'And what makes a kid like you think you can play the psychiatrist?' Adam asked tersely.

Her lips trembled and she bit them angrily. 'You don't have to be as old as Methuselah to know that a life without love can be a pretty miserable business.'

He looked away from her burning gaze and stared at the luminous eastern sky.

'Sometimes one experience can be enough for a lifetime,' he said with monotone finality.

Clare was silent. She had tried. He was as resistant to the idea of marriage with anyone as he was to her. She had got nowhere except a whole lot further on the road to separation from him. Maybe she had even spoiled the last short days with him . . . ruined the only thing she would take away from Sicily—her memories.

Adam had found a pressing need to re-tie the laces of his walking shoes. When he had finished, he stood up with sudden decision and held out a hand to pull her to her feet.

'I'll tell you what, though,' he said with determined cheerfulness, 'if I ever do change my mind, I'll ring you up and tell you you weren't such a kid after all.'

Her hand was like ice in his warm grasp, and she was suddenly aware of what a grey, barren, lifeless place the mountain-top was.

'Where are your gloves?' asked Adam, rubbing her frozen hands between his.

'I dropped them up at the crater, and the wind blew them over the edge,' she said tonelessly. 'There was nothing I could do about it.'

'Put this one on.' He pulled off his right glove.

'Then you'll be cold.'

'No, I shan't. Put it on.' He waited, then pulled her in to his side, took her left hand in his right, and buried both in the furry pocket of his sheepskin coat as they began to walk over to the jeep.

Hands . . . That's what Sicily will always mean to me, Clare thought bitterly. Hands were not enough at the side of all she longed for from this man. She snatched hers away and pulled off his glove, thrusting it back at him.

'You're making us look plain stupid,' she said. 'And in any case we're going to be in the jeep in a second. I'll survive.'

'Silly girl,' he said mildly. And she felt it, for any number of reasons.

They were heading back to San Paolo that day, Clare thankful to be driving and occupied. The road ran close to the Ionian and then the Tyrrenian Sea, skirting the edge of the province of Messina and bringing them to Palermo province.

At Cefalu, they stopped for a cooling swim, parking above the end of the beach, from which point they could see the sweep of the bay and the dramatic view of the huge cathedral dwarfed in turn by the massive pine-studded rock against which the town huddled. The daytime crowds were drifting away from the main beach, and the golden sand was deserted at their end.

Clare tore off her dress and ran thankfully into the sea, Adam close behind her. For a while they had a totally enjoyable time, swimming along parallel to the shore and back.

'I think that's enough,' said Adam when they reached the point where the car was parked. He started in to the shore, then paused and trod water, looking back. 'Aren't you coming?'

'Not yet.' His assumption that he had only to say the word and she would instantly obey aroused chidish rebellion in Clare. She had been floating contentedly on her back, but now she turned over and swam determinedly out from the beach.

She had not gone far before she got her come-uppance. Cramp attacked with vicious suddenness, knotting her leg with pain, making her cry out involuntarily and beat the water with her arms in panic. When she felt her left arm muscles go into spasm too, blind fear gripped her, and it was Adam's name that she cried out.

He was there almost at once, supporting her, holding her against his blessedly firm floating body until the spasm relaxed, leaving her limp and exhausted and more frightened than she cared to admit.

'Better now,' she gasped.

'Relax, then. I'll get us back to shore—if you try swimming you might trigger off another attack. Let yourself float against me.'

Hands gripped her waist so that she leaned back, her head against Adam's chest, aware of the strong thrust of his legs as he swam the two of them back towards the shore.

'You can let me go now. I can manage the last few yards,' she volunteered when they were close to the beach. But he didn't release her until the water was shallow enough for her to stand, waist-high, facing him.

'Not the sort of experience to go in for too often,' she said ruefully. She was breathless from something that could be shock or fear, but was equally likely to be contact with the magnificent body she couldn't help staring at.

A strand of her hair, dark with sea-water and sending a little runnel of water down into the hollow of her breast, was trailing forward over her shoulder. Adam reached out a finger and lifted it away from her flesh, moving it delicately back. His touch lingered on her with the effect that, though she had come to expect it, still electrified her. She thought that if she looked down at her shouder, the mark of his touch would be emblazoned on it.

'How's the leg now?' he asked.

'Still feels a bit unreal—tingling, you know.' So was the rest of her, for that matter, and it wasn't cramp that was causing it.

He led her out into shallower water, then crouched down and kneaded the muscle of her calf, his fingers expert and gentle as they coaxed life back into her leg. His dark head brushed against her as he knelt there, and as Clare looked down on it and on the brown shoulders studded with shining drops of sea-water she ached to clasp him to her bare midriff, to plead with him to love her. It would be easy, she wanted to say. She could love him enough for both of them. Some of what she felt would transmit itself to him in time. She knew it would.

The effort to control her emotions made her shiver, and Adam looked up into her face, then stood and put his arms round her, hugging her against the warm strength of his chest.

'You little fool . . .' he said, but tenderly, 'You could have drowned.'

'No, I couldn't . . .' Clare murmured into the bronze velvet of his skin. 'You were there.'

He let go of her. 'That trusting nature of yours will get you into trouble one of these days.'

Is there more trouble than this? Clare wondered. 'Maybe,' she said, looking up at him. 'Or maybe I'll learn . . . In any case, I haven't thanked you yet. But I do. I was very frightened. So—thank you.'

His eyes scanned her face, smiling at her wide-eyed seriousness.

'I think I'm entitled to demand that you do it a little better than that.'

He pursed his lips for a kiss, comically, no doubt thinking she needed cheering out of her nervous reaction. It would have been stupidly awkward and obvious to refuse.

Clare closed her eyes, afraid of what he might read in them, then she reached up on tiptoe, keeping a careful distance, and kissed him. It was the lightest of kisses, when she was longing to fling her arms round his neck and cling to him.

Unexpectedly, Adam's arms tightened round her, refusing to let her go down from the tips of her toes, holding her against him for a long moment, then he said roughly, 'That wasn't much of a kiss for a life,' and his mouth claimed hers with sudden demanding hunger, so that a reckless wildness made her first respond with a blaze of feeling to match his own, then tear her lips away from his to say, panting,

'You see! You're not immune, are you?'

He raised his eyebrows and his look took in every inch of her scantily clad body.

'What man would be, in the circumstances?'

Clare stamped a foot and the water scattered up between and around them.

'You know what I mean! You pretend you want to live like a monk for the rest of your life—'

'A slight exaggeration,' he interrupted. 'When this subject—of which you seem inordinately fond, incidentally—was last raised, we were talking about marriage. I assure you, Marjorie Proops the second, that when I'm feeling the antithesis of monk-like, to put it delicately, I don't exactly have to sit at home feeling frustrated. On the other hand, nor do I have to make for the nearest church or register office. Could we now consider the subject closed and my needs adequately catered for?'

Clare ran blindly out of the water and picked up her towel, hiding her head in it. She should never have said that, of course. What on earth was happening to her? She was practically flinging herself at this man who really couldn't make it more obvious that on any serious level at all he wanted none of her. She wanted right now to burst into tears of frustration and incredibly painful sadness at the speed with which time was running out and going back to England was hurtling towards them.

Adam was towelling himself briskly when she risked a peep, and his face looked closed and frowning.

She couldn't bear the thought of the two weeks ending in a horrid atmosphere as well as heartache. She dragged together the remnants of her self-respect and began to make harmless general chat about the prospect of a message from Marcella and the shopping they ought to do before getting back to San Paolo.

Adam answered her civilly enough and the trek around the first supermarket they came across helped as a distraction, but it was a fairly silent drive from then on until they reached Montenico just before Castellammare.

The village was ablaze with flags and flowers and coloured lights to be switched on later, and it was obvious from the air of thronged excitement that it was *festa* time.

Adam questioned a passer-by through the window as they crawled along at walking pace, diverted along side streets because the main road was closed in preparation for the horse-racing through the village. It was the last evening of the *festa*, the big night, he was told.

With the nearest they had been to the former easy atmosphere, Adam turned to Clare and asked, 'Want to come back and see what's going on tonight?'

She glanced quickly at him. 'That would depend on whether there's a message from Marcella, wouldn't it?'

'Even if there is, I wouldn't do anything tonight, in any case.'

'I'd love to come back, then.' The way Clare felt now, a solitary evening in San Paolo would be hard to get through. The more people to distract her, the better.

There was no message waiting at the house. Adam's shrug was unexpectedly philosophical. 'I'll go over there tomorrow in any case—it's make or break time. But if I have to go back having achieved damn all, being miserable tonight won't help. So get your glad rags on.'

Clare wore her brightest frock—a pagan print of bold and unexpected colours that should have sworn horribly at each other but instead created a kind of wild magic. There was a matching narrow scarf, gauzy and long. She tied it round her forehead, knotting it at the side and letting the ends float down with her hair. Dangling jade earrings picked out one of the dominant colours of the dress.

She looked totally different. She *felt* different, a little dangerous. She flashed a challenging smile at her reflection. These two weeks couldn't be allowed to fizzle out. Let them go out with a clash of cymbals.

Adam's eyebrows acknowledged that her appearance had impact.

'At least I shan't lose you in the crowd.' he said, the throwaway words contradicted by the way he looked at her as she walked towards the door.

All the world seemed to be out strolling through the streets of Montenico, and the atmosphere was intoxicating. Somewhere a band was playing boisterously. Clare recognised snatches of Verdi and Mascagni over the laughter and voluble chattering of the crowd. The church front was bright with hangings, balconies were transformed with flowers and palm leaves into exotic vantage points for women and children. In the main street sawdust was strewn and the crowds were restricted to the sides, penned in by brightly painted barriers and controlled by busy officials wearing brilliant red sashes.

Adam bought peanuts and nougat from persuasive salesmen wandering through the throng with trays, then they were accosted by a man with a different kind of tray, more like a miniature village or maze.

'What does he want?' asked Clare.

'He's a sorter out of lives.' Adam darted a mocking glance at her. 'Should be just up your street, if you can manage to hold back and let somebody else do it for a change.' He gave money to the man, who removed a tiny mouse from a box under the tray and put it in the glass-enclosed world of the maze.

Adam translated as the man interpreted the significance of the mouse's wanderings in and out of the little streets and buildings, and Clare gathered that her fortune was being told. Travel, riches, the usual blessings were predicted, then the mouse began running excitedly in and out of one particular enclosure while the man counted, the crowd around laughing and joining in.

'*Uno, due, tre, quattro, cinque——Cinque——*' The next word Clare didn't understand, and Adam, joining in the laughter, made a dismissive gesture with his hand while he tried to edge her away.

'Five what?' Clare persisted, and someone in the crowd called out,

'Baby, *signora. Cinque figli*!' pointing with delight to Adam and herself.

Clare felt herself blushing and yielded to Adam's pressure to move on. She was still wearing the ring—it had become an accepted part of her personal landscape now. It wasn't surprising that they had been treated as man and wife by the fortune-teller.

'What can you expect from a mouse and a doll's house?' Adam said laconically. 'Look, the parade's beginning. Let's get a good view of it.' He insinuated them into a small gap, pushing Clare to the barrier in front of him.

Horses, brightly saddle-clothed, went by, prancing delicately as their riders reined them in. Each horse had nodding plumes on its head and coloured ribbons woven into its elegant tail. The crowd cheered their favourites, and one of the red-sashed men, giving a commentary through a loud-hailer, said something that caused a roar of laughter.

'What was that?' asked Clare.

'He was telling the riders and spectators not to look up at the ladies on the balconies, out of courtesy.'

Clare saw that there was a mock-modest pressing in of skirts among the ladies in their eyries. She doubted that the advice would be heeded. There had been enough sly pats and strokes on various bits of her since they mingled with the crowds to indicate that inhibitions were non-existent in Montenico tonight.

The horses had disappeared now, and tension was fizzing high through the crowd as they anticipated the start of the races.

Suddenly a dog—a little griffon—ran out into the road, stopping bemused at the roars of protest from the crowd, then darting in one direction and another, not knowing which way to go.

The crowd, wild with excitement for the coming race and the bets placed upon it, turned in an instant from good humour to ugliness. Someone threw a stone, then another flew from the opposite side of the road, the dog yelping and whimpering, cowering while the missiles and the shouting intensified.

Clare had at first frozen in disbelieving horror at this cruelty on a public scale she had never before encountered. As the dog whimpered, she was galvanised into action. She squeezed through a gap in the barriers and ran out to scoop the little animal up, only then realising as she fell back towards the barrier and Adam's hands pulled her roughly over the top that thundering hooves were charging wildly down the street, swerving to avoid her and sending sawdust flying up into her face, the wave of heat from their bodies taking her breath away. Had she been a second later, she might not have lived to see the horrified anger on Adam's face as he blazed at her, 'You fool!'

Before he could add more, a young girl in black pushed towards them, crying with relief and repeating, '*Molte, molte grazie, signora*!' through her sobs as she took the dog from Clare's arms and hurried back into the house behind them. Around them the men in the crowd were talking excitedly and looking with none too pleasant expressions in Clare's direction, their comments undecipherable, she was relieved.

'We'd better get out of this while we can,' Adam said under his breath, leaning over her with feigned attentiveness while his fingers bit into her arm as he steered her through the crowd and into a side street.

Clare was weak-kneed with reaction. 'They'd have killed that dog, or let the horses do it,' she said through chattering teeth.

'And the ones who think you responsible for their favourite horse not bringing in the prize money would no doubt be equally ready to kill you,' said Adam. 'A fat chance there is of blending into the crowd with you in that get-up. You might as well carry a banner!'

When they were safely back in the house at San Paolo, she turned to him.

'I'm sorry. I don't know what else I could have done—but I didn't want to spoil the *festa* for you.'

He was looking at her very strangely, and suddenly acting even more strangely still. He was pulling her into his arms, leaning his head on hers, his hand moving compulsively up and down the curve of her back.

'This time you really could have killed yourself,' he said gruffly, his voice smothered in her hair.

Clare thought wildly that he couldn't do this to her again . . . reduce her to putty in his arms, and then act as though it had never happened as he had done at Cefalu.

She pushed against his chest. 'Let me go, Adam. I'm in no mood for playing around.'

'Can't you tell the difference between fun and reality?' he said thickly. 'This is real, Clare, whether I want it to be or not, heaven help me.' Then he was kissing her with a hunger that was unmistakable, and the sharp tug of response from deep inside her put an end to any further protest she might have attempted. For a long moment they clung together, then Adam was raining kisses all over her face, snatching off the scarf still tied round her forehead, impatient with its frail barrier, saying wildly,

'Call it proximity—holiday madness—a million and one things . . . but tonight when for that ghastly second I thought you were going to be run down—oh, Clare! I couldn't have borne it if that had happened.'

The surge of joy that blazed through Clare obliterated everything but desire for the urgent sweetness of the moment to last for ever.

He might be trying to explain his feelings away, but at the same time he was giving her such undeniable proof that she *did* matter to him—she wasn't just anybody who happened to be there. It was something. And it was wonderful. She luxuriated in his embrace, aware of the delicate, obstinate flicker of a flame of hope at the heart of the stronger heat of passion he aroused in her.

With cruelly inappropriate timing there came a pounding on the door that tore Adam's lips briefly from hers, but only to say fiercely, 'Damn whoever it is! Ignore it.'

But whoever was there at that hour would not be ignored. The knocking went on, insistent, determined.

With a muffled groan Adam gently loosened her arms from his neck. Clare slipped into the kitchen as he went to the door, knowing that her flushed skin and lips would be a blatant advertisement of their interrupted lovemaking. From there she heard, and understood, the visitor's first words, and realised with a sinking feeling what their effect would be.

'*Buona sera, signore. La signora Rafaeli e ritornata . . .*'

There was more that Clare could not understand, but it was enough to know Marcella was back.

When the door closed again she went slowly back to Adam. It was as though she had left the set of one stage play and was now going back into another entirely different one, she thought with a touch of hysteria. Adam had changed, as though he had never, for that one unbearably sweet moment, been the lover she had longed for him to be.

He had already collected an armful of papers and he was making for the stairs.

'Lock up, will you, Clare?' he said distractedly.

'I've got things to do for tomorrow . . . and then I must grab some sleep. We had precious little last night. You gathered that Marcella's back? First thing in the morning, I'll tackle her again. It's now or never.' His voice faded away as he disappeared upstairs. Clare might as well have ceased to exist, except as a sounding board for his thoughts.

Torn between laughter and tears, she went over to close the shutters. Along the track she saw a match flare and a cigarette glow against a shadowy face. Probably the man who had shattered her dreams, pausing on his unthinking way, oblivious of the part he had played in her life.

Tears won the day, blotting out the sight of him before she closed the shutters and then groped to put out the lights one by one.

She felt that, before, she had only skimmed the surface of frustration. Now she really understood it.

CHAPTER SEVEN

IN SPITE of the long day it had been, with the small-hours start on the Etna trip, Clare couldn't sleep. She tossed and turned, her hopes alternately soaring as she remembered the urgency of Adam's arms round her, then plummeting at the recollection of how quickly his attention had switched from her to work. She went over and over the few words they had exchanged before they were interrupted, and although at the time they were spoken they had seemed full of joyful conviction, by the time morning sunlight was glowing round the gaps in the shutters all Clare could read into them was that Adam felt like kissing her because he wouldn't have liked her to have died while in his care—a pretty obvious and thoroughly unremarkable reaction, really.

And if he had not enjoyed being interrupted while doing so—well, what aroused male does welcome distraction at such a time?

She could endure her bedroom prison no longer. Quietly she got up and put on her bikini and sun-dress, grabbed a towel, and crept downstairs and out of the house.

The tide was out as far as it ever went—no more than eight or nine feet. Clare swam slowly towards the end of the headland, careful to keep within her depth after yesterday's scare. Going further than last time, she found that the point of the headland had double arms of rock reaching out into the sea and enclosing a tiny sheltered bay, pristine and inviting.

She climbed carefully over the rocks out of the water and made the first footprints of the day on the unblemished sand, feeling like the only woman in the world—and as lonely.

She was not alone for long. Giving her the feeling of an action replay, a familiar little grey dog came trotting through a gap in the rocks, bustling over to her, its big eyes bright and friendly.

'Unless you've got a double, we've met before. What are you doing here? Not in more trouble, surely?' said Clare, bending down to stroke the rough little head, the black moustache coaxing a smile out of her. 'Anybody's friend, aren't you?' she went on, squirming away from the enthusiastic tongue that was finding her face now that she had crouched down.

'Not anybody's, but certainly yours.'

The voice startled her. A woman in a white robe was standing in the gap through which the griffon had come, a towel wrapped turban-like round her head. At first Clare didn't recognise her. Only when the woman moved forward did her walk and the proud poise of her head identify her as Marcella Rafaeli.

Clare stood up, smiling. 'Good morning. Is he yours?'

'Yes, still mine, thanks to you. I saw your——' Marcella smiled '—I can only call it a foolhardy gesture. But I'm so thankful that you made it and were not hurt in the process. I am eternally in your debt.' She held out her hand and clasped Clare's. 'I was on my cousin's balcony, unable to do a thing. Giuliana's maid sneaked out to meet her friends, and Sam followed her.'

'Sam? It suits him.'

'One of my souvenirs from America . . . He was a gift from my husband—so you see he is very precious to me. I intended to seek you out and thank you today. But *your* husband—he must have scolded you for risking your life for a dog?'

Clare's cheeks flushed at the title given so naturally to Adam.

'He did, rather,' she admitted.

'And especially on what could be your honeymoon? Is it? You are so very young.'

'No—a business and pleasure trip.' At least that answer was truthful.

'And I have made a poor contribution towards the success of the business side.'

Clare's heartbeat quickened. Marcella had brought the subject of the interview up. She must be very careful not to say anything that could prejudice things further. She looked into the older woman's face, her grey eyes sympathetic. 'Adam has been disappointed, yes. But he told me what you said . . .' Frowning in concentration, she repeated the Sicilian proverb. '*Chu cerca lu picchi ntà li cosi trova spinanzi chi rosi*.'

'He taught you that? So . . . the man has a heart hidden beneath that oh, so persuasive businessman's façade!' Marcella picked up Sam, rubbing her cheek against his rough head, and walked one or two paces, preoccupied. Then she turned. 'I owe you a big debt. I take it that whatever makes your husband happy gives you happiness too?'

'Yes . . . of course.'

'Then come over to the *palazzo* with him. He shall be told what a good, kind, sweet young wife he has—so that he knows to whom he owes his good fortune—and then he shall have his interview.'

Clare knew that Adam would feel like killing her for what she was going to say now, but she had to do it for the sake of her conscience.

'And the thorns you spoke of, *signora*. What about them?'

Marcella smiled. 'After so many years, they are not so sharp. It is right that the story should be told and the picture painted in its true colours. I shall not change my mind again.' She put the dog down. 'And now I must get out of this wet bathing costume and make myself as beautiful as an old woman can be before I tell my story. Come at ten.' She paused, and the first trace of imperiousness manifested itself. 'And you will not allow the impossible man to try to send you away this time. I have always had more reason to trust women than men. I wish you to be there.'

Clare watched her go, then scrambled back over the rocks and swam along to the path up the cliff as quickly as she could, eager to tell Adam the surprising news that would make his day.

She heard him before she saw him, shouting at her from the top of the path.

'Where have you been? How do you imagine I felt when I saw your things on the beach and no sign of you? The last thing I needed was to start this day with a mad panic!'

'Well, I'm here now—and I couldn't very well tell you where I was going when you were still asleep, could I?' Clare flew up the last bit of path and stood facing him, her eyes sparkling with the secret she was about to reveal.

'Ever heard of pen and paper? And you needn't look so damned smug. After what happened at

Cefalu you might have shown more sense than to go off swimming alone.What if you'd got cramp again, and this time with nobody around to lug you ashore?'

'I'm not a fool, Adam,' she said pityingly. 'I swam close to the beach—well within my depth. I would have been back sooner, but I saw that dog again—the one from last night's *festa*.' She paused, prolonging the pleasure of telling him about Marcella.

He scowled. 'And that's another death-wish episode I don't particularly want to be reminded about.'

'Not even if I tell you that he belongs to Marcella? And that she's very, very grateful?'

Now she had his full attention. The navy-blue eyes were alert.

'What exactly are you saying?'

'That you're invited to go along at ten o'clock this morning and do your interview with a lady who's very glad to have her dog with her still.'

A slow smile was spreading across Adam's face.

'You crafty little witch!' he said admiringly.

Clare's own smile faded. 'What do you mean, "crafty"? I did nothing crafty at all. Marcella is genuinely grateful. If you must know, she said that she supposed what pleased my husband would please me—and so you could have your interview.'

'Told you the husband and wife thing made sense,' he said smugly.

'Oh, you're impossible!' Clare pushed past him. She didn't know what she had expected, but certainly nothing like she'd got.

In two quick strides he was by her side, stopping her.

'Clare, I'm delighted. Truly.'

'You've a jolly odd way of showing it.'

'Believe me. It's what we came for, and I'd almost convinced myself it wasn't going to work out. It's just that coming on top of finding that you haven't after all gone and drowned yourself, nothing seems quite as important.'

She snorted derisively. 'And coming after last night, that stretches the bounds of credibility.'

Adam looked genuinely puzzled, and she wished she had never referred to last night.

'What do you mean?' he asked.

She shrugged. 'I mean that I could have been walking off a cliff or under a bus when you heard Marcella was back. I ceased to exist between one second and the next.'

'But you were perfectly all right then. Where was the danger?'

'O-o-o-h!' She practically growled her exasperation. 'I'm going to make some coffee.'

'What a good idea.' He followed her into the house.

'And by the way,' she added, 'Marcella insists that I go along this morning. I didn't fish for the invitation. She said that she trusted women more than men, and I can't say that I blame her.' Clare crashed the crockery around, getting rid of a bit of personal steam.

When Adam didn't answer, she sneaked a look at him over her shoulder. He was staring at her, but not seeing her, his mind running on some private track.

'Did you hear that?' she asked impatiently.

'I heard. Tell me, you got on well with Marcella, didn't you?'

'She's extremely nice.'

'I don't mean *you* liked *her*. I mean *she* liked *you*.'

'Because of Sam—yes, I suppose so.'

'She wouldn't have insisted you went to the house just for that reason. She'd have sent you flowers or something. No, she's taken a shine to you. Clare—' he came up to her and she could tell that all his business engines were working at full throttle, 'how would you feel about playing interviewer—putting my questions to Marcella? It really would help from my point of view . . . and if she took a liking to you, as I expect she did—who wouldn't?—she might relax that little bit more.'

'You're suggesting that a raw novice like me might actually help an experienced actress to perform? Isn't that just a little bit ridiculous?'

'Not ridiculous at all. You'd be surprised how unsure of herself an actress can be when she hasn't got somebody else's words to put across. I'm serious.'

'But I wouldn't know what to ask—and how could I in any case? Isn't there all the business of Equity cards?'

'I don't mean to leave you on the film—that would put the cat among the pigeons. No, we'd dub in professional questions afterwards. The camera would be on Marcella all the time. You'd just be—'

'The bait? The one likely to squeeze the most out of her?'

He nodded, unmoved. 'The one to deliver the goods—as I'm sure you could. Will you do it?' He was looking at her with a half-smile, his eyes searching her face, and when he looked at her like that she felt she would do anything for him, no matter how much she disapproved of his motives.

'I'd be right there all the time, obviously,' he coaxed. 'If you didn't follow a line I wanted taken up, I'd join in. All you'd have to do would be prompt a bit—be a good listener.'

He was just using her, as he would use anyone to achieve his purpose. She knew that the fact that she was the person involved was immaterial really, and the knowledge tired her.

'I don't have much choice, do I?' she said shortly. 'It's what I'm here for, after all—to do what you require done. So you can take it that I'll earn my wages. And now I'm going upstairs.' She paused in the doorway. 'And if you have any misgivings—which I doubt—you may be interested to know that I reminded Marcella of her roses and thorns statement, and asked her if she was sure now that she wanted to do this.'

'Good,' said Adam with annoying satisfaction. 'If she didn't change her mind there and then, she's really going through with it this time.'

'You are so unscrupulous . . .' Clare said slowly, looking at him.

He raised his eyebrows. 'Single-minded is the way I'd prefer it put. Off you go!'

Soon after they arrived at the *palazzo* Marcella took Adam off round the garden to choose a place for the interview, since he wanted to film out of doors with a backdrop of the coast and sea.

Clare, sipping her glass of chilled wine, watched them from the table under a pergola shady with vine leaves. Marcella was wearing a bronze dress, elegantly simple and flowing, patently the product of some Italian couturier. Pearls glowed in her ears and at her throat. Watching the older woman move, her hands illustrating her words, Clare felt depressingly ordinary in her yellow cotton dress. Adam had seemed part of Marcella's world as he kissed her hands in the most natural way when they arrived. The only asset Clare felt to have was youth—and so far that hadn't done much for her.

The objects of her reflections disappeared round the side of the house, and after a while Adam came back, fizzing with energy.

'There's a balcony overhanging the sea round there—pots of pelargoniums . . . and railings that give a good view of the sea and coastline . . . if I sit Marcella against that, it's exactly what I want.'

Clare felt suddenly overwhelmed with nerves.

'Adam, I hope I do this right for you.' She had stretched out a hand towards him, needing some kind of reassurance, but he was caught up in the momentum of his ideas.

'You'd better!' he said, not even looking at her as he hurried her round to join Marcella.

Once the initial camera test was done and checked on the screen, and she had got over the strange experience of hearing her own voice sound quite composed, Clare began to feel a bit better. Adam had gone over a number of key questions with her, and at his signal she began with the first one from his list.

'What was San Paolo like when you lived here as a girl?'

'You perhaps think it is a quiet place now. I can only say that you should have seen it before the coming of the motorway.' Marcella gave a little moue of disapproval. 'In the old days life passed us by, here. Things were done as they had always been done—from as far back as the Middle Ages, it seemed. And heaven help the one who wanted to change them!'

'Did you want change?'

'Not at first. When I saw Vito and fell in love with him, I would have been happy for everything to take its course in the old way.' Marcella looked enquiringly at Clare. 'You know something of our marriage formalities?'

'No.' Clare shook her head. 'But I'd like to.'

'It will seem unbelievable to you. Until I became unofficially engaged to Vito, I never actually spoke to him—that wasn't allowed. I knew of his interest in me in the way one always does know such things. He would walk past my balcony in the evenings with this friends, and there were looks that I pretended not to see . . . Eventually I had a letter from him asking me to become his fiancée, and I sent him my answer—following the traditional way of expressing such things, of course. We didn't even have the freedom of the secret written word! But it didn't matter . . . only Vito mattered.'

'You said "unofficially engaged". When did the engagement become public?'

A shadow seemed to fall over Marcella's face. 'In our case, never. When Vito came to my house to ask if our two families could meet and formalise our engagement, there was such rage as I had never seen on my father's face. He told Vito never to cross his threshold again. It seemed that an uncle of Vito's, many years before, had been involved in the death of my father's cousin. The families could never come together as we wished them to do.'

'How could you accept that something happening years before you were born, maybe, should determine the course of your own life?' Clare asked with feeling.

'We didn't.' Marcella's simple answer startled both Clare and Adam. Clare heard his slight intake of breath behind her and knew that now they were coming to the real story that Adam wanted.

'You mean you defied your families?'

Marcella nodded. 'An aunt who was sympathetic acted as messenger between us, or we could never have arranged anything—my parents watched me like guards in a prison. My aunt gave us money; her own fiancé had died and I think she regarded our romance as her own. I ran away with Vito and we were married in a little village beyond Cefalu where Vito had found a new job.'

'You were married?' This had not shown in the research done by Adam's team.

'For weeks only.' Marcella sighed, her eyes clouded with memories. 'I was young . . . With Vito I was so happy, but always hanging over us was the shadow of my family's displeasure, and that caused me much sorrow. In the end, Vito said he would go and beg my father to accept him. He did it for me . . . and I never saw him alive again.'

Clare was beginning to suspect the awful ending of the story.

'He met with an accident?' she prompted gently.

'No accident.' Marcella's eyes met hers, dark with sorrow. 'My father killed him—my own father. He took Vito's body to a cove the smugglers used for their shipments of doctored wine to the mainland. Everybody knew what went on. My father had only to start a rumour about Vito's connections, and village gossip did the rest. Nobody knew that I had married Vito. My family would not even admit publicly that I had gone to him. They said I had gone to work in Palermo.'

'But how did you find out what had actually happened?' Clare had forgotten the camera, Adam, everything, in the emotional impact of the story.

'My father came and told me.' Marcella said with cold simplicity. 'When I hurled the accusation of killing his own son-in-law at him, he turned away from me, saying that he had neither son-in-law nor daughter. Those were the last words we exchanged. I never saw him again.'

'I'm so sorry . . .' Clare leaned towards Marcella, her face full of sympathy, not quite knowing what to say. Marcella smiled and lifted her head proudly.

'It was a long time ago. The years alter many things—not least one's own viewpoint.'

Clare was still imagining how Marcella must have felt at the time.

'I can understand why you went to America,' she said. 'But what made you want to come back?'

'Partly a desire for the truth to be told. At the time I had no real choice but to let Vito's name be dishonoured. What else could I do? How could I betray my own father, no matter what he had done, and know that it was my word that brought down on him the consequences of his actions? But now I can no longer hurt him, and I am strong enough to tell the truth. That is my first reason.'

'There are others?'

'A simple desire to end my days in the country that gave me life. To lie near Vito in death as I did for so short a time in life. There have been other men . . . but no love is as sweet as the first.'

Clare nodded slowly. Words seemed superfluous.

'And as I said . . .' Marcella went on reflectively, 'one's viewpoint changes. During my years in

America, I saw so many marriages break up—including one of my own. I saw children confused and frightened, parents deeply hurt by what their sons and daughters did. In the end, though I could never forgive what my father did, I came to understand and even to respect a little the belief in family that prompted his action.'

Clare was very much caught up in the discussion by now, and with her own circumstances at the forefront of her mind, she began to ask Marcella questions that Adam had not anticipated—about the nature of love, and the hold of family loyalty.

Adam must have changed his position without her noticing, because she was quite startled when he spoke from somewhere behind and to the right of her.

'Coming to the end of the tape now.'

She turned quickly to face him, embarrassed at being so carried away.

'I'm sorry, Adam. You should have stopped me.'

'No reason to. That went quite well, I think. Many thanks, Marcella. May I go indoors again and play it through? Then, if it seems all right from my point of view, you can come and check that you approve. You said everything you wanted to get across?'

'Even more.' Marcella smiled at Clare. 'I shall take this persuasive young lady to see my orchids while you are busy, Adam. So much talking!' She stretched elegantly, then rose, holding out a hand to Clare.

The talking, Clare soon found, was not over.

'I have been much concerned with the truth,' said Marcella when they were out of earshot of Adam, 'but this, it seems to me, has nothing to do with truth at all.' She took Clare's hand and fingered the wedding ring lightly.

Taken completely by surprise, Clare couldn't deny it. Her eyes met Marcella's and she shook her head slowly. 'No, I'm afraid not. Adam and I are not married. But how did you guess?'

Marcella gave a brief laugh. 'A new bride doesn't ask all those questions about the nature of love, nor does she express so many doubts as to whether it is possible to know that it is real. She knows all the answers!'

Clare began to feel distinctly uneasy. If Marcella had picked up so much from their conversation, what exactly had Adam captured on tape?

'Did I sound so very transparent?' she asked.

'Not only did you sound it, you looked it.' They had reached the glasshouses and Marcella turned to her orchids. 'And now you must look at my blooms. Beautiful, aren't they?'

She quoted Latin names and histories of each plant, but most of it went over Clare's worried head. Her concentration was sadly lacking.

'Are you lovers, then?' Marcella had switched tack again with startling suddenness. 'I can ask this so personal question,' she went on, 'because I am certain that the answer will be no.'

Clare shrugged hopelessly. 'Right again. Actually I'm no more than a temporary employee of Adam's. He said that San Paolo would not approve of our sharing a house, no matter how innocently, so some degree of pretence was politic.'

'You are not lovers . . . but you would like to be?'

Clare could only flush with embarrassment at once again having her feelings so correctly read. It was impossible to be angry at Marcella's questions. She had been honest about her own life, and there was something appealing about such directness.

'It seems I don't need to tell you anything about my feelings . . .' she said in rueful admission.

'Then, as one who has suffered and enjoyed much through love, let me urge you not to deny your feelings. Don't question them into non-existence. Trust them.'

Clare looked into the dark eyes. 'But what if there's no hope of feelings being reciprocated? Adam doesn't know I exist . . . except when I can be useful to him in some way.'

'I think you—'

Adam's voice interrupted, calling across the garden. 'Ready to run it through for you now, if you'd like to come.'

Whatever Marcella thought was to remain unvoiced. With some trepidation Clare followed her into the cool interior of the thick-walled Palazzo.

As Adam had promised, the camera focused on Marcella, her fine face reflecting the emotions of what she was saying, silhouetted against the wildness of the savage coast.

But when the conversation began to wander unto uncharted territory after Marcella's story, the camera wandered too. Clare saw her own face in shot, in profile, serious, and even to her own eyes vulnerable and revealing.

'But, having known Vito for so little time and at such a distance, how could you be so sure that you loved him? Surely love can't flare up as quickly as that?' she watched herself ask, knowing that she was thinking not only of Marcella and Vito but of her own feelings about Adam.

Marcella's face was on camera again, looking into her own with gentle understanding. Too much understanding . . .

'If you have to question your feelings, then you don't love. When you love, you know. It's as simple as that.'

Then Adam's quiet voice announcing the end of the reel, and Clare's own face looking directly at the camera—directly at Adam, her feelings towards him caught in revealing close-up.

The screen flashed and went blank.

'Perfect from my point of view,' Adam said briskly. 'Anything you want edited out, Marcella?'

'Nothing.' The older woman looked at Clare. 'We can leave everything in Adam's capable hands, I think, don't you, my dear?'

When they left Clare expected and dreaded some more personal comment on the day's shoot from Adam, but all he said was, 'That's that, then. No more hanging around. We can leave for home tomorrow. You did well, Clare. You coaxed far more expression from Marcella than I would have done on my own. I can use that bit at the end—cut it into the real interview . . .'

He went on analysing the film and its contents, and Clare realised that what she had been saying and how she had been looking didn't matter at all. All he had had in mind while he watched the film was which bits of the conversation could be vandalised to enhance the film proper. As she had told Marcella, for Adam she definitely only existed in so far as she was useful to his job.

And the job was over now . . . so, from this moment on, she ceased to exist altogether.

CHAPTER EIGHT

CLARE had a magazine open in front of her, but she was not really reading it. Through the windows of the plane she had watched Sicily dwindle into a golden blur far below, and she had felt as though she was leaving part of herself behind.

Adam was as quiet as she was, but, of course, for entirely different reasons. Clare knew that he had not slept well the night before. She had been lying awake for ages herself when she heard him go downstairs. She slept a little, fitfully, after that, waking later to get up and lean out of the window and gaze her fill for one last time at the moonlight silvering the calm sea, and to breathe in the scent of thyme and mint that would for ever, she knew, evoke for her this time and place.

It wasn't until she saw the tiny glow of a cigarette in the direction of the garden wall that she realised Adam was there. She hadn't known, even, that he smoked; it was the first time she had seen him do so.

Clare shrank back hurriedly. She had no desire to be invited down for further discussion of the hows and whys of the film that was so obsessing him. She couldn't have borne it—when all she wanted to do was cry out, 'What about me?'

He had been preoccupied while they ate a hurried breakfast and loaded the car. The drive to Punta Raisi had been a brooding affair, the thoughts of both of them turned inward.

Now Adam had been scribbling incomprehensible notes in his Filofax—enough to keep both him and his staff busy for weeks, it seemed. He apparently couldn't wait to be back completing his film, and nothing else found a corner in his mind.

Clare swallowed, but the ache in her throat stayed stubbornly put. What shall I be doing twenty-four hours from now? she wondered. She seemed incapable of constructive planning. All she could think was that in a matter of hours now she would be leaving Adam, once she had collected her things from Monk's Eden. And then where would she go? The prospect of accommodation and job-hunting seemed far more bleak than when she had first left home such a short time ago. It was almost a shock to remember that first leaving—so important at the time, and now so faded in comparison with the leaving that was to come.

She forced herself to make one or two concrete decisions. She would go straight to London. If there was somebody in the company flat, she would book into a hotel for a couple of nights, and then . . . The short burst of mental activity fizzled out into depression again.

'Are you all right?' Adam had put away his papers.

'Fine, thanks.' One more social platitude to add to the rest.

'You're not very talkative.'

Clare shrugged. 'I've nothing to say at the moment. In-flight inertia, probably.'

The stewardess came round with drinks. A dreary film flickered without meaning on the screen. The plane's engines throbbed on.

'Clare——' Adam said suddenly.

She opened her eyes. 'Yes?'

'Would it be possible for you to stay on for a couple of days? At Laveham, I mean. I'd like a typescript of the soundtrack of Marcella's interview done so that I can work on shaping that section of the film. You'd find it easier to do than someone strange to the thing.'

The request to stay on had Clare's heart leaping at first, but as Adam explained his reason for asking her she was filled with a sense of hopelessness. It was only putting off the evil hour, and she didn't think she could take it.

'I'm sorry, I'm afraid I shall have to leave at once when I've collected my things,' she said.

'Why will you?'

'I shall have work to go to.'

His blue eyes looked disbelievingly at her. 'How can you have? You had nothing fixed when we came away.'

'That doesn't mean I haven't put in dates to the agency and a request since then.' She hadn't—but she wasn't going to drag out the torture any longer.

'I'd *like* you to do it. We work well together.'

Clare hardened herself against the persuasion in his voice.

'Any competent audio-typist would do the job as well as I could. You know that,' she said reasonably.

'Aren't you interested in seeing the finished film, then? Surely you'd like to do that?'

His persistence and his utter blindness to what she really wanted sharpened Clare's determination not to give in.

'Of course I'm interested—but I shall be able to see it on the TV, shan't I? I'm sorry, Adam, but I really do want to get on with finding a permanent job. And I *have* done what I said I'd do.'

He crossed out a note he had made with a stroke so fierce that it ripped the page. Clare looked out of the window and pretended not to see. The flight dragged on.

'Suppose I offered you a permanent job?' Adam said suddenly.

'And sacked your poor secretary for nothing more than being unfortunate enough to get 'flu? That's a non-starter of an idea, isn't it?'

'There are other slots at Breckland. Of course I wouldn't attempt to sack anyone.'

'Adam,' Clare said with finality, 'you said yourself that I needed to get into a more appropriate job than being a secretary. I think so too. So let's drop the subject, shall we?'

Adam got up impatiently and disappeared towards the back of the plane. Clare just had time to notice that his eyebrows were at their most demonic. She felt very tired and hoped he wasn't going to resume his attempts to get his own way when he returned.

He sat down again in silence, however, but he kept looking at his watch and shifting his long legs around restlessly so that eventually she was forced to ask him if he was feeling all right.

'No, I'm not!' he said with smothered savagery. 'Who the hell would be, in these damned circumstances?'

Clare gave him a pitying look. 'All because of a little typescript?'

'I don't give a damn for the typescript!' He spiked his hair with both hands, staring wildly at her. 'I've been trying as I've never tried in my life to control what I feel. I spent most of last night on that futile exercise—but I'm damned if I can keep it up. Clare,

I know this is crazy, and I know we've only known each other for two short weeks, but this flight's nearly over, then there's only a short drive to Lavenham and before I know it you'll be walking out of my life. Clare . . . I don't want it to end. And that's the plain and simple truth.'

She looked at him, scarcely breathing, her eyes wide with incredulity that she was afraid to allow to flower into belief.

'Say something!' he pressed her. 'We'll be landing in less than a quarter of an hour. Tell me I didn't imagine the way you were when I kissed you . . . the way you looked yesterday when we were filming?'

Clare's feelings won the battle with her fears. Happiness began to shine in the depths of her eyes. 'You didn't imagine anything, Adam,' she said unevenly. 'But you . . . I thought I wasn't even on the same planet in your eyes. I thought——'

'I can imagine what you thought,' he interrupted, 'because it was what I wanted you to think. I was afraid of my own feelings, Clare—I still am. I've had years of suppressing them, it seems.'

She moved impulsively towards him, then remembered where they were and sank back in frustration. 'Oh, Adam!'

'I know. There's nothing I want more than to kiss you right now. I choose the damnedest places, don't I?' His mouth twisted in a wry smile, but his eyes were saying everything she wanted to know. He took her hand in his and circled her wrist with his free hand, sliding his fingers up the satiny skin of her arm and making her flesh tingle under his touch. Then, glancing over the back of the seat to make sure he wasn't overheard, he went on seriously, 'You know a bit about my life, Clare. You asked if I'd ever marry again, and I was pretty definite in my answer—far more definite than I feel now. But I want to be honest with you. After Fay, I thought I'd never allow another relationship to cause me so much pain. No more lifetime vows suddenly cut off and meaningless. It hurt too much. Work was safer; it would always be there. Part of me still clings to that idea. But then you walked into my life and began to penetrate all that carefully constructed armour I'd encased myself in.' He looked seriously into her eyes. 'What I'm trying to say now is that it may still be too soon to be definite about the future. That's what I want to be quite open about. I want you to stay around . . . I want that desperately. I want to give this chink you've made in my defences time to grow and widen to let you permanently into my life. Is it asking too much of you to accept that? Is it enough to stop you walking away from Monk's Eden and never looking back?'

Clare squeezed his hand, her grey eyes luminous. 'It's enough. I'll stay, Adam. I know my mind, truly, I promise. I'll——'

The man who had been sleeping soundly in the next seat suddenly awoke, making some remark about the patch of turbulence they were going through and which Clare had not even noticed.

She closed her eyes while Adam listened patiently and politely to accounts of flight horrors from his neighbour. It didn't matter. Nothing mattered now that she knew she had not been imagining the compelling tug of feeling between herself and Adam. She was flying home not to emptiness, but to the hope of some kind of future with him. On the strength of hope like that, she could manage to tolerate, even to sympathise with the poor bore in the next seat but one.

She would make Adam love her without reservation. She knew she could do it. All she needed was the chance and his eagerness to try . . . and that she had got.

The flight home turned from bad dream into promise of happiness.

Monk's Eden was lovely in the late afternoon sun. As Clare parked under the archway, she saw that a motorbike was standing outside the kitchen door.

'That's my brother's,' said Adam. 'What on earth is Chris doing here?'

As they got out of the car, Mrs Kaye came hurrying through the doorway, a tall, dark-haired boy in jeans and a red sweater following her. He was unmistakably Adam's brother, but without the marks life had scored on Adam's face.

'Oh, Mr Melvin, I'm so glad you're back!' Mrs Kaye exclaimed.

Adam pressed her hand. 'I should have rung you from the airport, but I didn't think, I'm afraid. Too much on my mind.' His eyes met Clare's with secret warmth. 'What's this villain doing here? Looking for a free doss-down, are you?' He thumped his brother goodnaturedly on the back, then pulled Clare forward. 'Meet Chris,' he said. 'Chris, this is Clare.' He didn't explain her, but Clare was tinglingly aware that he kept his arm round her shoulders as she shook hands with Chris.

'Your brother's here because I asked him to come. Oh, dear!' sighed Mrs Kaye, and Clare realised that the housekeeper was looking decidedly unlike herself. Adam realised it too, but Chris forestalled his question.

'I'll tell him, Mrs Kaye. Why don't you make some tea? I expect they could do with some.'

'Tell me what?' Adam's expression changed. 'Is something wrong at home?'

'No. Mum and Dad are fine. It's this end where there's been trouble—a break-in, I'm afraid, Adam. That's why I'm here.'

Mrs Kaye was still hovering in the doorway, her face anguished.

'I only went over to my sister's for the day, Mr Melvin. In broad daylight, they got in—broke a window in the courtyard. Had all the time in the world to do it, I expect, and nobody to overlook them. I should never have left the place. I blame myself bitterly for that.'

'Katie, don't be silly,' Adam said with kind composure. 'You had every right to go out for the day, and you know it. Now be a love and do as Chris says—make us that tea, will you? Nobody is blaming you. Chris will tell me all about it. Go along, now.'

Chris pulled a sympathetic face when the housekeeper had gone.

'Rotten homecoming for you both. I haven't even asked if you had a successful trip.'

'We'll answer that later. Come on in and tell me what's missing.' Adam led the way into the house.

'That's a bit of an imponderable until you've checked through the place. Some things were obvious and Mrs Kaye knew they were gone—silver photograph frames, pictures, a lot of the small antique pieces—things she was used to seeing and caring for. But they went through your desk, and neither of us knew what was in that. And the bedrooms were turned inside out—the one you were using too, Clare, I'm afraid.'

'Unless they wanted clothes, they wouldn't find much of interest in mine,' said Clare.

Adam was ahead of them looking round the sitting-room.

'A bit bare everywhere,' he commented. 'But I imagine it looked far worse than this when you were called in, Chris. You must have done a lot of clearing up. Thanks for that. I was a bit premature with my rude remarks.'

'Mrs Kaye was very upset. I thought I'd better stay on until you came back—she's still nervous.' Chris went over to the fireplace and handed a paper to Adam. 'I've made a list. The police want you to add to it and ring them as soon as you're sure you've got everything down.'

Adam read through it. 'Quite a haul.' Clare could imagine what he was feeling. First his wife, and now so many of the tangible reminders of their marriage gone. She ached for him, though he was putting on a bold front and gave no sign of the distress the burglary must be causing him.

'What can I do?' she asked.

Adam looked up at her. 'Nothing much here, I don't think. I shall just have to go through everything myself.' He smiled at her, and she marvelled that he could manage to do so. 'You'd better cast an eye over the room you used. He might have been a transvestite, you never know!'

Mrs Kaye brought in the tray and Clare poured tea for them all, then took her own cup upstairs, leaving Adam and Chris to get on with the unpleasant task of checking what else was missing.

It was not until she was actually in her bedroom, looking at the forced lock of the suitcase that had been in the wardrobe and was now lying open on the bed, that she remembered. There had been something very much worth stealing in the pocket of the case. Giles's ring.

Hurriedly she put down her cup and felt in the elasticated pocket. Nothing. She began to take all the clothes from the case. Nothing was as she had left it—the things had all been refolded and put back, by Mrs Kaye, no doubt. Whoever had broken in had had his pick.

She unfolded and examined everything. Every handkerchief was opened and shaken, every pair of tights unrolled and felt. But all the time Clare knew how useless it was. If he had emptied her case, then he had found the ring.

All the same, she still went over every inch of the wardrobe and the bedroom floor in the desperate hope that the ring could have dropped unnoticed and rolled into some corner unobserved.

When she finally admitted to herself that the ring had gone, all the implications of announcing its theft crowded into her mind.

She was going to have to tell Adam that her engagement ring was missing when he hadn't the least idea that there had been an engagement for a ring to represent. Then she would have to tell him how recently she had broken it off.

Clare shivered at the thought of what that would do to the fragile bud of their relationship. How much faith would Adam have in the truth of her feelings for him in the light of such a recent involvement with another man? 'I know my mind, truly——' she'd said on the plane. What validity would that statement hold when Adam knew about Giles?

She thumped the floor where she was still crouching.

'Damn, oh, damn! Why did I ever come away with the wretched ring?' Giles was going on affecting her life, it seemed, through she couldn't blame him for this.

She sat thinking while she heard Adam and Chris going round the other bedrooms, and then going downstairs again, their deep voices fading away into the ground floor of the house.

Pale with dread, she steeled herself for the task of telling Adam and went downstairs after them.

Adam looked up from his desk and read her expression instantly.

'What is it, Clare?'he asked.

She swallowed. 'They did get something of mine. A ring—an engagement ring.'

Instantly he was on his feet and crossing the room to put his arms round her.

'You poor love! The swine got your mother's ring, did he? That's awful. I'm so sorry.'

Her head was pressed against Adam's chest and, conscious of Chris watching, Clare hesitated, then let the wrong assumption stand. She would tell him about Giles, of course she would, at the earliest private opportunity—but at this moment fate had offered her an easy way out of a tricky situation, and she could see no harm in taking it.

'This has got to be done,' Adam was saying gently as he led her over to the desk and settled her in a chair from which she could see Chris's lively interest in a relationship he was only just beginning to appreciate. 'Can you give me a description of the ring, love?'

Clare swallowed. 'It was a yellow diamond—emerald-cut, claw-mounted, eighteen-carat gold. Size L.'

Adam finished writing and reached for the phone. 'Better get this business over with, then we'll eat. Perhaps you could have a word with Mrs Kaye on that subject, Clare?'

He was sparing her the unpleasantness of listening to him reporting the loss of what he thought was her mother's ring, and Clare loved him for his sensitivity while at the same time being consumed with guilt for arousing it so wrongly.

Mrs Kaye was busy taking food from the freezer. Vegetables were already prepared.

'I'll have a meal ready in half an hour. I feel better when I'm doing something,' she told Clare. 'Awful to have a thing like this happen when I was alone in the house. I really had locked everything up properly, you know, Miss Vincent. The man who repaired the window can vouch for the fact that they had to break their way in.'

'Adam doesn't blame you—of course he doesn't. And neither do I,' Clare told her.

Mrs Kaye stopped dramatically. 'Don't tell me they took something of yours as well?'

'A ring. I shouldn't have left it in my room—shouldn't have had it with me, for that matter. Don't start apologising, please!' Clare gently silenced the housekeeper's words before they were spoken. 'It just isn't your fault. Here, let me wash up the tea-things. I'm looking forward to one of your meals. You know what airline food is like!' She deliberately went on chatting until she felt that things were calm again, then, when she had finished the dishes, she walked out into the garden, thinking that Adam and his brother might like the chance to talk in private for a little while.

The grass had grown since Adam had last

trimmed it on the eve of their departure for Sicily. It looked incredibly green to Clare's eyes, which were still full of the golden dryness of Sicily. She sat on the bank of the moat, watching the swans. The cygnets had grown too in the two weeks they had been away. She tried not to think of the awfulness of having lost Giles's ring. Which would annoy him most? Losing her or losing the ring?

'Funny little beggars, aren't they?' Chris squatted down on the bank beside her. 'Incredible to think they'll end up like their elegant parents.' He whistled a few bars of the 'Ugly Duckling' song, then turned to Clare. 'So what's going on between you and my brother, then?'

'What do you mean?' Clare stalled.

'Come off it—I wasn't born yesterday! There's more than a business arrangement.'

Clare pulled at the grass. 'I've known your brother for exactly two weeks. You can't make much out of that.'

'I've known my brother for twenty-three years—and I know what my eyes tell me. Two weeks or two years—the evidence would be the same.'

Clare capitulated to some extent. 'I can't tell you anything definite, honestly. We've enjoyed each other's company, and we want to go on doing so. That's all, really. You know how your brother's been feeling for a long time.'

'Too right.' Chris tossed a pebble into the moat. 'And it's about time it stopped, if you ask me.'

Ripples from the pebble spread across the moat. A window opened and Adam looked out. 'Dinner's ready, you two.'

'Coming!' called Clare. She lowered her voice for Chris. 'You won't say anything to Adam, will you?'

He grinned at her. 'Well, that shows you're serious, anyway! And Adam would be a fool if he weren't. Come on. I'll keep my mouth shut—big brother would probably thump me if I didn't!'

Laughing, they went in.

In view of the fact that Mrs Kaye had not been told of the exact time of their return, she and the microwave came up with a very good meal. There was home-made pâté, then beef olives with garden peas and asparagus and tiny Jersey Mid potatoes bright with butter and parsley, followed by a creamy, tangy lemon mousse.

Surprisingly, Adam seemed more or less unmoved by the robbery, and the subject was either avoided or completely forgotten. Clare loved watching him and his brother together. Their banter and teasing revealed a side of Adam she hadn't known, and she looked forward—no, *hoped*, she corrected herself guiltily, afraid of tempting providence, that one day she would meet all his family.

The phone rang, and Adam went off to answer it. When he came back a few moments later, the subject of the robbery was again centre court.

'Someone from the CID is coming round in a short while, I'm afraid. They want to check on one or two details. Not a very peaceful homecoming, is it?'

They took coffee through to the sitting-room, the carefree atmosphere dissipated by anticipation of the coming visit. Clare helped Mrs Kaye, under protest, to clear the dining-room. She felt a certain apprehension about speaking to the police. Would they ask her to repeat the statement about the ring? Had Adam actually said to them that it had belonged to her mother? It wasn't a pretence that materially affected anything, but all the same it was a deception that made her feel uncomfortable. What complications came hot on the heels of the slightest deviation from the truth!

Inspector West was a poker-faced man, very correct in his manner, but Clare felt that there was something threatening about him. Probably it was due to nothing more than her own bad conscience. He ran through Adam's additions to the stolen items, eliciting further identifying details, then turned to Clare.

'Now, Miss Vincent, I'd like to ask you a little more about this ring you've reported missing.'

Her heart bucked as he spoke, and while he went on to check the description Adam had phoned in she was very much on edge, but no mention of the ring's origins was made, and gradually she relaxed.

'Any particular identifying marks you can think of?' He looked steadily at her.

She had not mentioned the engraving inside the ring. 'There are initials inside,' she said. 'I forgot to mention them. GER.'

Giles Edward Rushton, his mark, she was thinking distastefully. If she had forgotten to mention them it was probably because she had always felt angry about Giles's attitude.

'Now that's very strange . . . very strange indeed,' the inspector was saying reflectively. All three of them looked at him expectantly. 'An affair of odd coincidences, this is turning out to be,' he added with maddening slowness.

Adam was frowning. 'If you know anything about the ring's whereabouts, I'm sure Miss Vincent would appreciate your sharing the information with her.'

'Oh, I'll do that, sir,' the inspector said blandly.

'Here's the first coincidence. One of my men was going round the jewellers in Ipswich, engaged on quite another enquiry. He was in the back room of one particular place—fairly well known to us—going through the safe and the books, when he happened to look up and saw someone come into the shop and get the word to buzz off sharpish. My man naturally prevented this, being of an inquisitive turn of mind, and found that the fellow was intending to sell a ring such as you've described—down to the last detail.'

'Oh! That's a—' Clare had been going to say that it was a relief, but she saw that the inspector had more to say.

'Yes, you might think that would be good news for you, Miss Vincent. So it would be, but for another coincidence. Our computer shows that another such ring, identical in every respect, was reported stolen in Walberswick two weeks ago.'

Under his steady scrutiny, Clare felt her heart begin to thud. Giles! What a fool she had been not to tell her father that she still had the ring. Of course Giles wouldn't delay in reporting it missing. What a fool she had been, a confused fool. Adam was looking both uncomprehending and annoyed that he didn't understand what was going on. Chris looked plain intrigued. The inspector's eyes remained unblinkingly fixed on Clare.

'Two identical rings,' he went on. 'Right down to the initials inside them. We have to decide, do we not, Miss Vincent, which one is yours before any rejoicing can be indulged in? Or do I have to ask myself a rather tricky question? Could there have been an even stranger coincidence? Could a ring—one ring—be so unfortunate as to be stolen twice—once in Walberswick, and once in Lavenham? You see what I mean?'

Clare saw. He had not said it in so many words, but he was implying that she might be the first of the two thieves. Before she could speak, Adam was rising from his chair, flying to her defence.

'Inspector West, I don't know what confusion has arisen here, but I must tell you that the ring Miss Vincent lost belonged to her mother and is of great sentimental value.'

'No, Adam.' Clare had to speak out, but she was terrified.

'What do you mean—no?' Adam stared at her.

'I mean that it wasn't my mother's ring. You assumed that at the time, and I—I didn't want to have to explain where the ring really had come from.'

'What are you saying?' It was Adam who spoke, but all three men were staring at her, beginning to think her capable of heaven knew what. Clare felt as though she was drowning in a swamp of her own making. She dragged her eyes away from Adam's.

'I can explain everything. There is only one ring—but I certainly didn't steal it from Walberswick, Inspector. It was——' Clare's eyes met and fell away from Adam's dark blue intensity, 'it was my own engagement ring, nothing to do with my mother, and I should never have let it be thought that that was so. Two weeks ago I walked out of my home in Walberswick, leaving a note for my fiancé breaking off our engagement. I told him in the note that I was enclosing the ring. I was . . . not very calm at the time, and I forgot to do so. Everything happened very quickly after that. Mr Melvin offered me the job of driving him on an assignment which meant leaving the country. I didn't think it wise to take the ring abroad, but equally I didn't want to tell my family and my former fiancé what I was doing. So I left the ring here, and it was stolen: only once, Inspector—not twice. I can give you names of people with whom you can check this story, but no doubt one of them would be that of the person who reported the ring stolen in the first place—Giles Edward Rushton. I—I'm sorry. I've been both careless and very foolish. I'm sorry.'

Clare looked at Adam as she said the last two words, dreading what she would see written on his face. But prepared as she was, it was still a dreadful shock to see how grey he had gone under his tan. He was looking at her as though she were a stranger—an odious stranger. The intensity of his reaction stunned her. It was worse, far worse, than she had anticipated.

'Adam——' she began helplessly, knowing that she could not begin to talk to him in front of these two men, but pleading for understanding and forgiveness with her eyes. Then she realised that the men were not looking at her, but at the doorway through to the hall behind her.

Mrs Kaye spoke apologetically. 'I'm sorry, Mr Melvin, but this gentleman says he's with the inspector. He insisted on coming in, though I said you were engaged in an important meeting.'

Clare turned, and was appalled to see Giles coming past the housekeeper into the room. Her voice croaked his name, barely audibly.

Giles looked quickly round the silent group, his colour high, his eyes flicking angrily past Clare, then coming back to settle on her.

'I asked you to wait in the car, sir,' the inspector

said curtly.

'I've waited long enough, Inspector, two weeks, in fact, and now I'm entitled to an explanation. First there's the little problem of what you've done with my property?' he said to Clare, then he looked scathingly at Adam and Chris. 'And then there's the question of which of these two chancers you've been frolicking around Europe with.'

'Giles!' Clare exclaimed.

Adam came forward, towering over Giles's slight figure, and Clare stepped quickly between them, but Adam was making no move to hit Giles. He spoke with perfect control, his voice iron-hard.

'I concede that you have a point, though your manner of making it lacks a certain courtesy.' Without looking at Clare, he spoke to her. 'Perhaps you'd like to take your fiancé into the study. No one will disturb you.'

There was nothing else she could do but obey him. Clare led the way from the silent room, Giles hot on her heels. It was Adam she wanted desperately to talk to, not this man who felt like a stranger to her.

With a physical pain in her chest she remembered Adam's expression when she had looked at him at the end of her explanation to the inspector. He too had turned into a stranger in that instant. Would he ever let himself trust her again?

'Why, Clare?' Giles demanded passionately when the study door was closed behind them.

She was asking herself the same question, though not for the same reason.

CHAPTER NINE

'YOU don't really need an explanation,' said Clare, facing Giles's heated face as calmly as she could. 'You had my letter, and I tried to tell you often enough before that that I didn't feel able to go through with marrying you.'

'Your father didn't believe you any more than I did.'

'I know. That's why I had to get away from both of you. It was the only way I could see of doing what I knew to be right for me.'

Giles stared ferociously at her. 'I suited you very well as long as it was convenient. As long as you needed some mug who wouldn't fuss if dates were cancelled at the last minute—who'd sit around with your family and try to pretend it was exactly what he wanted to do.'

Clare's eyes stung with tears. 'That's not fair, Giles! You know my mother's health meant that my free time was unpredictable.'

'I don't call it particularly fair that you made use of me for as long as it suited you, then dropped me like a hot potato as soon as you got the chance to spread your wings.'

'That just isn't true. If things had been right between us I wouldn't have left. But they weren't, Giles, surely you know that?'

He turned his head away stiffly. 'They were right for me.'

'But not for reasons that matter. It was appropriate

to be engaged to the daughter of your partner. Fine to be marrying the other half of the business.'

His eyes met hers defiantly. 'What's wrong with finding that satisfactory? Property has always featured strongly in the best marriages.'

'Best financially, maybe. What about romantically?'

Giles snorted contemptuously. 'Romance! Is that what you were after with the toffee-nosed giant through there? If so, it doesn't look as though you met with much success.'

Clare felt her telltale cheeks giving her away. 'I was not looking for romance, I was looking for work. Adam happened to need a driver and I took the job. Getting out of the country suited me, and got me away from you and Dad—but . . .' To her annoyance the tears threatened again. She had never been a weepy person and it infuriated her that she was showing this weakness in front of Giles.

'But he wasn't slow to take advantage of the fact that you were ready to go off with a stranger at the drop of a hat!' he sneered. 'Is that it?'

'He took advantage of nothing!' Clare told him fiercely. 'He's more of a gentleman than you'll ever be if you live to be a hundred!'

'Suffering from a bit of frustration, are you? I got the impression that he didn't regard engagement-breakers with the greatest favour—so it looks as though it'll go on.' Giles was probing around, seeking out her vulnerable spot to inflict as much pain on her as he could.

'I'm sure you're right about Adam's feelings. He knows what it is to love somebody and lose them. He probably attributes his feelings to you—he has no idea how misguidedly.'

They stared at each other, eyes blazing, then Giles folded his arms.

'He certainly seems to be the current knight in armour in your eyes. Two weeks after dashing away from one relationship you're up to your neck in another. Tell me, Clare, if you weren't in your right mind when you got involved with me—what state of mind are you in now? How long is the present illusion going to last?'

Giles was needling her in spite of herself. He would never talk her round into thinking she should go back to him, but the way he was going on about the speed of her falling in love with Adam was getting right under her skin. Not that she supposed there was any love on Adam's side right now. That session in the sitting-room had put paid to any feelings that might have been growing in him towards her. And she had only herself to blame. Clare's shoulders drooped miserably.

'I think you'd better go, Giles. All this mud-slinging isn't getting us anywhere. I'm sure you'll get your ring back from the inspector—and that was what you really cared about, wasn't it?'

The bravado seemed to go out of him. 'If you really think that was all I cared about, then you obviously didn't have any of the necessary feelings for me.'

She stepped towards him and put her hand on his arm.

'Oh—I'm sorry, Giles. We've said some silly, hurtful things to each other. You were good to me . . . so many, many times. I shouldn't have let myself get mixed up between gratitude and love. But I do know the difference now. And gratitude isn't enough for a marriage.'

For a moment the hostility died in his eyes. 'I just hope for your sake that you're not every bit as mixed up now as you were then. What are you thinking of doing?'

'I shall finish the work I've agreed to do, and then go. To London, maybe.'

He looked hard at her face. 'You look different.'

'I am different. I've—this sounds silly, but I feel I've grown up a lot over the past few weeks. I've still got a long way to go, though. I really am sorry to have caused this messy situation, Giles. I hope things work out for you.'

He rejected her tentative sympathy instantly, his face stiffening again, the short-lived moment of non-combat over.

'You don't have to concern yourself about me, Clare. I'd say from the brief glimpse I've had of the set-up here that you've enough problems of your own to keep you occupied.'

She refused to join battle again. 'Tell my father I'll phone him as soon as I can.'

Giles's eyes condemned her. 'He hasn't got much reason to be grateful to you either, has he? Don't come with me. I'll find my own way out.' He walked past her without a goodbye.

Clare felt exhausted. She didn't want to face the inspector again and could see no reason for doing so. If he really needed to speak to her he would come and get her. She sat near the study door, conscious of comings and goings through the hall, and eventually of a car starting up.

She was just wondering how she could manage to speak privately with Adam when the door opened and he came in. Clare got up.

'Adam, can I talk to you? Without Chris around?'

He looked at her, then, without answering, went and poured her a stiff brandy.

'You'd better drink this. You look as though you need it.'

She took the glass, her eyes on his expressionless face.

'It wasn't easy with Giles. He was very angry.' Her teeth chattered against the glass and the brandy burned its way down into her stomach. Adam was looking so impersonally at her, and though her throat was burning she felt icy cold inside.

'You've got to let me explain—please,' she begged.

'I presume you've done the only explaining necessary—namely to the man involved. It's quite obvious to me if not to you that your complicated life only brushed against mine. It was never on the cards for us to become more deeply involved.'

'But you said—I thought—I want—' Clare was so afraid that the words wouldn't come.

He looked at her with devastating coldness. 'I don't think you have the least idea in the world what you want. Let's drop the whole painful subject.'

'I should have told you about Giles. I don't know why I didn't. I mishandled the whole business.'

'A feminine prerogative,' he said shortly. His face looked so *closed* to her.

'It wasn't a question of walking out on him suddenly, you know,' she urged. 'I tried to tell him how I felt loads of times, but he wouldn't—'

'I've told you, it's your own private business. You must sort it out as best you can.'

But you are at the heart of my life now, Clare wanted to cry out to him, but how could she when he looked so icily detached, and every word underlined the fact that he had drawn a line under their relationship?

The phone rang and Adam went over to the desk and picked it up.

'Adam Melvin . . . Oh—John. Hello . . . Yes, this evening.' He listened for a moment, then his face broke its stony mould to express feelings at last—feelings of outrage. 'They can't do that! . . . All right, you tell me that they have—but they don't know what they're writing off. Listen, John—I've got the Rafaeli interview . . . Yes, the Rafaeli. That's where I've been . . . Never mind how. It's got to be included in the film—it's far and away the most dramatic bit of material we've stumbled across . . . Well, when have you fixed the damned meeting for? . . . Hell! I can't possibly have the thing edited for then.' He listened with half an ear and pulled a train timetable towards him, flicking over the pages with one hand and then running a finger down the times. 'Listen, John. The only thing I can do is bring the film up to London as it is and run it through for them at tomorrow's meeting. If they can't see then that it's worth waiting for, then I'll accept that they're mad and wash my hands of it.'

Clare, listening miserably, didn't understand how Adam could become so instantly caught up in his business. The only explanation must be that he didn't care enough about anything that had happened between them. Panic rose in her throat. She was losing him. With every second he was getting further and further away from the closeness that had flowered with such promise between the plane and this ill-fated return to Monk's Eden.

Talk of times and places went on, then Adam put the phone down. He turned to Clare again, his face draining of animation at the sight of her.

'Do you intend staying on to do the typescript I asked you about?'

'I promised I would,' she said dully.

His look was eloquent. It said more clearly than words that her promises were not to be trusted.

'In that case I'll run off a copy of the soundtrack for you to work from. You'll have gathered that the *Roots* sponsors have brought the deadline forward. If I hadn't got back today I'd have been too late. With luck, tomorrow I'll talk them into waiting for Marcella's interview to be edited in.'

Work obsessed him again. He was talking to himself rather than to her while he slotted a blank cassette into the sound recorder and started winding back the Marcella tape in the video.

Clare stepped forward in desperation and pressed the 'stop' button.

'Adam, you can't do this! You've got to listen to me. You must try to understand. I've been all kinds of fool, I know. But the Giles business wasn't the sort of thing to tell you at first—you've got to admit that. And once I really knew you, I—' she swallowed hard '—I forgot everything.'

'Surprisingly quickly. And what about when you "remembered"—which I presume you must have done when you found the ring missing? At that point it seems obvious to me that what might, in the light of a blue moon, pass for absent-mindedness became then and there something a little less excusable.'

Clare felt to be shrinking in size as his icy gaze shrivelled her.

'I didn't want to have to tell you like that, because I was forced into it by circumstances . . . and with Chris there.'

'You didn't want to have to tell me—period. That's

more likely. And why? *I'll* tell *you*. You didn't want to tell me because if you had a mind at all—which seems debatable—you haven't made it up now any more than you had when you were involved with that Giles fellow.'

'That's not fair! My mind is absolutely made up. But yours isn't, is it, Adam?' she said hotly. 'You're glad to be able to shrink back into your tight little shell, because for you there'll never be anyone to match that wonderful, perfect Fay of yours.' She realised what she had said, and stepped back. 'What am I doing? I'm sorry, I shouldn't have——'

'But since you have——' he cut in '—I may as well disillusion you on that score. You are *exactly* like Fay. She too entered into a relationship and changed her mind. *She, too,* wasn't comfortable with the truth and preferred her little intrigues to go undetected and undiscussed. *She, too,* left her "goodbyes" in note form in order to avoid the unpleasant task of explaining herself in person. Oh, you come very close indeed to being a carbon copy of my "wonderful, perfect" wife!'

Clare stared at his livid face, speechless with the horror of what he had just said. There was no questioning the truth of it. It was etched in pain and anger on his features. He had overturned her whole idea of his past . . . shattered it and re-formed it into a sickening image of how he saw the present to be.

Oh, she could understand Adam's reaction now. Everything was explained if Fay had really been as he had said. His reluctance to commit himself to anyone else, his total rejection of herself now that he thought she was another woman in Fay's mould . . . everything fell into place.

The impossibility of fighting against such a tide

of loaded odds overwhelmed her, imprisoning her in the silence of a despair so total that she couldn't find a single word worth saying.

Adam was pointedly indicating that the conversation was at an end. He switched on the video again and turned his back on her.

'I shall leave the tape on my desk,' he said tightly. 'You can work in here. Paper's in the cupboard under the window. I shall be on my way to London before you're finished. I shall be most grateful for your help.'

Every word hit her like a blow. Such cold, organised politeness left neither room nor hope for love.

Clare groped behind herself for the door-handle and backed out of the room. When she had shut the door, she leaned against it, her eyes closed, scarcely able to think what to do and where to go.

Chris's voice recalled her from limbo.

'Clare——' She opened her eyes to see that he was coming through the hall with the inevitable tray of tea-things. Tea—the panacea for all ills . . . but nothing could lift her out of this pit of misery she was engulfed in. Chris saw, and reacted to the degree of her distress. 'Come and have some tea. Please . . .' he said.

She followed him into the sitting-room, too devoid of initiative to do anything else. He put down the tray and looked at her with boyish embarrassment. 'Rough time?'

'Pretty rough,' she managed to say.

'Who was worst? The "ex" or Adam?'

Clare swallowed. 'Both bad. Giles didn't pull his punches, but Adam . . .' Suddenly she crumpled into a chair, hiding her tears in her hands. 'Oh, Chris—at first he wouldn't talk . . . and then, when he did . . .'

Chris hovered over her. 'Look here, don't get so worked up about it. I've been on the receiving end of Adam's displeasure more times than I've had hot dinners. It blows over. Give him until tomorrow to calm down.'

'Tomorrow he won't be here. He's going to London—someone rang up,' she said.

'I know.' Chris was pouring the tea. 'I picked up the phone at the same time as Adam did and heard the first part of the call.' He looked into her eyes as he handed her a cup of tea. 'Drink this. You look like death.' He watched while she sipped the hot liquid, then went on, 'Tell me to shut up if you want to . . . but what about this Giles person? Is it really over with him?'

'It never really started in any true sense. It was no more than one huge mistake that needed drastic action to get me out of it. I can't go into the details now, Chris. You'll have to take my word for it.' Her voice shook again, and Chris hurried to say,

'Of course.' He shot a quick look at her, then looked carefully down into his cup as he said, 'You've got to concede that it must have all been a bit of a surprise for Adam, though. Coming like it did, I mean, with police inspectors and burglaries and things.'

Clare nodded slowly. 'Oh, I concede that, all right, though I didn't understand his reaction fully until he told me what his marriage was really like. He compared my behaviour to Fay's, in fact—said I equalled her in instability, untruthfulness and sheer cowardice. I don't think I shall ever forget that particular moment.'

'You mean you didn't know until then just what

things had been like between them?' Chris started to grin and then quickly stopped himself. 'Communication's been a bit lacking both ways, hasn't it? But he's out of order in his comparisons—absolutely. Fay was a disaster, really—a complete butterfly. She needed to be constantly amused, and Adam, of course, had other things to do for a great deal of the time. He was certainly bowled over by her—most men were—but if he hasn't wanted to try again in a hurry it's because the first experience of marriage was such a bad one. That's the plain and simple truth of it.'

'What does he gain by letting everyone think the opposite?'

'Salvaged pride, I expect. Why should he broadcast the fact that he had a bad deal? I don't blame him for that.'

'But even Mrs Kaye, who lived under the same roof, seems to think it was an ideal marriage.'

Chris gave a cynical, reminiscent smile. 'Fay always managed to look as though she was in love with the man closest to hand. No doubt Adam got the full treatment for the time they spent together. What happened when he was working was anybody's guess, I imagine, but at least she kept whatever she got up to fairly discreet until . . .' He stopped, eyed Clare uncomfortably, then seemed to make up his mind. 'I might as well go the whole hog—but I'm relying on your discretion, Clare. I imagine that I'm the only person in the world to have heard directly from my brother's own lips that if his wife hadn't crashed her car that night, by the following morning she would have been on her way to Denmark with the man she was leaving Adam for. That was the message he got in the note she left him.'

'Oh, poor Adam!' Clare's eyes darkened with feeling, then flashed with outrage. 'A man like him! She must have been crazy!'

'But you're not. And you've just proved that you're far from indifferent. So you're going to stick around—I hope.' Chris took her cup. 'Give Adam time to calm down. Go to bed and sleep on it. He'll be a different man tomorrow. Furious tonight, maybe, because you have more of a past than you let him think. But that applies to him too, doesn't it? And neither past need have any bearing on the future. Don't be defeatist, Clare. I'm telling you in all honesty, my brother looked a different man when I first saw him with you this evening.'

It all looked so simple to Chris. But everything he told her only seemed to reinforce Clare's conviction that Adam wasn't going to envisage a future in which she played a part. Chris was only a boy, not yet able to understand fully the heights and depths of a man's emotions. He was looking at her now with such fresh-faced hopefulness—Adam without the darkness.

'Thanks for telling me, Chris, and for the tea,' she managed to say before getting up and going over to the door.

'Remember, everything always looks better in the morning.' His nice smile was twisting Clare's heart with his physical resemblance to his brother.

'I'll remember. Goodnight, Chris,' she said.

Upstairs in her room Clare sat on the bed and thought about all that she had learned—but with none of Chris's optimism that morning would find a miracle waiting to greet her.

Months had gone by before Adam had allowed

himself to get close to someone again, only to find that he had picked on a girl who had left a 'Dear John' letter behind her for the man in her life, just as Fay had done.

He had looked as if he hated her down there in the study . . . When he deliberately distanced himself from her like that, the world seemed to be falling to pieces around her.

Clare got up to close the curtains. The lights from the house were shining on the water of the moat. Adam's safe consolation—work—was continuing to occupy him. Lucky Adam. She had only her miserable thoughts to keep her company.

Even if she tried to explain about Giles to Adam now, she would only end up deeper and deeper in the mire of his disapproval. As Giles had made abundantly clear, accepting that she had not been in a stable state of mind when she got engaged to him did nothing to increase confidence in the reality of the love she had so quickly convinced herself she felt for Adam.

Giles's scornful expression kept haunting her. The trouble was, he had voiced not only his own personal scepticism, but the hidden doubts she herself felt. How could she be sure after only two weeks with Adam that she knew him and knew her own feelings well enough to trust them? What if she had merely been carried along on a tide of reaction to Giles and her family circumstances—a tide that would subside and maybe leave her stranded on another mistake of a relationship? The more she thought about it, the more insecure Clare grew.

Surely the sensible thing—and for goodness' sake, it was time she did something sensible—would be to give herself time to think. In any case, staying in

Adam's house until he decided to listen to her—or not—was not the most comfortable of situations. Chris seemed to think his brother would soon forget his angry reaction, but what did Chris really know of it?

Adam's opinion, Giles's opinion, her father's too, undoubtedly, once he knew about this latest development in her life, Chris's advice . . . all of it circled round and round in her mind. So many men, and all with such strong ideas . . . all of them telling her what was best for her.

Anger with the lot of them and with her own decision flooded into the void in her. She got up and packed her cases on the strength of it. She was going to leave . . . get away from all their questioning, advising, condemning voices. She would do the typing she had promised to do tomorrow morning, and be out of the house before Adam came back.

It was a relief to have made up her mind, and Clare felt drained of any other emotion.

Adam's taxi came and went while Clare was dressing. She heard the sounds, but resisted the urge to fly to the window on the stairs that overlooked the courtyard to see him. If she intended leaving—and she did—then she couldn't afford to indulge the slightest weakness.

Chris poked a bleary-eyed face round the study door while she was typing to ask if she wanted coffee. Clare didn't tell him her decision. The less time he had to work on her with his persuasive powers, the better.

It was as well she had left it to the last minute. The script finished and placed on Adam's desk, Clare told first Mrs Kaye, then Chris, that she was leaving. Mrs Kaye was easy, since she knew little of the undercurrents between Adam and Clare, but Chris fought against her departure every inch of the way.

From the house to the station—he had insisted on driving her in Adam's car once he found he couldn't prevent her going—he urged her to reconsider.

'Can't you see you're doing exactly what last night made him afraid of?' he said on the station platform, hanging on with dogged obstinacy until the very last minute.

'Then he won't be surprised. He gave me not the slightest indication last night that there was any point in prolonging this uncomfortable situation.'

'That was gut reaction. I've told you, he'll be a different man when he comes home today.'

'Chris, today began before Adam left for the station. If he had had a change of heart, wouldn't he have told me so then?' Clare detached herself from his restraining hand, thankful to see the train approaching. 'You're wasting your time—really you are. I know I'm doing the sensible thing.'

'But where will you *be*? You can't just disappear into thin air like this. Adam will kill me for letting you go.'

'Adam will probably be very thankful. You weren't there when I spoke to him last night.'

'At least give me an address.' Chris was trying to follow her on to the train, and Clare bundled him unceremoniously back on to the platform.

'I don't know where I'm going to be eventually, so there's no point. I shall go to my father's flat to begin with . . .' She tried to make a joke of it. 'The Isle of Dogs is quite appropriate, don't you think, for someone as much in the doghouse as I am. And it overlooks the river. Handy for suicide if I feel like it.'

'Clare!' Chris looked genuinely horrified.

'No, of course I don't mean that!' Doors were slamming. Clare leaned out and kissed Chris on the cheek. 'If I had a brother, I'd choose one just like you to fight for me. Goodbye, Chris.'

As the train began to pull away she saw the way he ran his hands through his hair above his anxious face, just as she had seen Adam do so many times. A mist of tears blurred the rapidly diminishing figure on the platform.

Clare sat down. She was not as tough as she had tried to appear to Chris. Nice Chris . . . so-like-Adam Chris . . .

CHAPTER TEN

SO BUSINESSLIKE she had been . . .

First checking that the flat was empty—the doorman reassured her on that score. A quick upward trip in the lift to fling open windows and leave her luggage, then there had been time to go along to a mini-market along the quay to stock up on the bare necessities.

A brisk shower and change into jeans and bright Benetton shirt—might as well look cheerful, even if you couldn't feel it—and another dash back to the newsagent's to get an evening paper for the job and flat ads.

Life was going on. She was going through all the correct motions, Clare congratulated herself. While she was in this achieving frame of mind, she dialled her father's number and told him where she was.

He asked one or two fatherly questions. Was she all right? Had she enough money? When was he going to see her? But on the whole he was more interested in talking about the Children's Book Fair that his company was taking part in the following week.

Well, that was fine. She wanted to be independent, didn't she? Not have anyone on her back—or on her conscience, for that matter.

'Is Giles all right?' she asked, associating ideas.

'He's nearly got everything sorted out to his liking. Monica Charlton was the biggest fly in the ointment—had to be talked round before she'd accept the cover design for her series . . . said she couldn't stand it at first, as usual.'

Her father went on at great length about Giles's difficult author as though there had never been a more personal area in which Giles had problems and which Clare might ask about. Clare listened with a wry smile. The men in her life—or should she say 'out of her life'?—were running true to form. Work, the great god, was supreme to all of them. Second to nothing.

She made a half-promise to spend a weekend in Walberswick next month, depending on whether she had settled a job for herself. She also established that the flat was not going to be required over the next two weeks.

There had been a definite step forward, she thought as she put down the phone. Her father had spoken quite pleasantly to her—no recriminations this time, and business the main topic. Back to normal, in other words.

Clare couldn't be bothered to ferret through the freezer stock for something to cook for herself, and she certainly didn't feel like going out to eat alone. She made a pile of toast, thinking guiltily that it was comfort food. So who needed comforting? she asked herself defiantly as she took it out to the balcony and settled herself on a lounger in the evening sun.

She had over-estimated her appetite and only managed a poor half of the toast. The noisy gulls, bobbing in the wake of every boat that passed, had the benefit of the rest.

She caught herself brooding and went purposefully to get the evening paper. There were a couple of flats that looked to be in possible districts but had utterly impossible rents. She would need to get people to share with her . . . people she didn't know . . . people who might turn out to be totally incompatible. It seemed a very futile was of organising one's life. Surely you should get the people you wanted to live with first . . . or preferably just one person . . . She was brooding again. She jumped up and indulged in a flurry of activity in the kitchen which didn't really need it and which would be serviced tomorrow in any case.

Back on the balcony, scanning the Jobs Vacant column, she found one job she could phone about in the morning and a couple of agencies to approach. There was nothing else she could do tonight.

She leaned on the railings, telling herself how lucky she was to be here, looking down on the Thames, a comfortable, even luxurious flat hers for the next two weeks. She really was *lucky*.

So why was she feeling so damned miserable? Once admitted, the truth made further pretence impossible. Clare sat down and faced up to what she had done under the guise of 'pleasing herself'. To begin with, she had certainly not pleased herself. She had made herself very unhappy. Here she was, miles away from Adam, trying to pretend that life was a bowl of cherries when it was a very bitter pill indeed.

She had listened to all their voices—Adam's, Giles's, Chris's—and run away from them. What she should have done was stand still and listen to the voice inside her, her own voice, the once she was hearing so clearly now. The one that was saying she loved Adam . . . would fight for him . . . make him understand and love her in return no matter how ill-disposed he might think he was towards her.

What was it Marcella had said? Not the taped words . . . Clare had typed those that morning, deliberately blocking her mind to them. No, it was the unrecorded conversation in the garden when Marcella had extracted the truth about the wedding ring that she wanted to recall now. 'Don't deny your feelings,' Marcella had said. 'Don't question them into non-existence. Trust them.'

That was where she had gone wrong. Too many questions. Too many doubts. Too much dissecting of the simple truth that just needed to be stated.

Clare went into the flat and looked at herself in the mirror. She saw big grey eyes, dark-shadowed now. A mouth that looked torn between smiles and tears. She leaned towards her reflection.

'I love him and I'm going back,' she told herself. 'I don't care how stupid it seems, how ridiculous I might look. That's what I'm doing, and that's what I want.' The face in the mirror was changing as she looked. Grey eyes could reflect the happiness inside as well as the skies above. This time it was her mind made up by herself. She was acting in response to her own feelings and not to a blend of sense and expediency.

She flung night things into an airline shoulder-bag belonging to her father. The cases could wait here, she wasn't going to tempt providence to deal her another blow by lugging them back with her. She hesitated a bit over the perishables she had bought at the mini-market, then decided to stick out her neck a little bit and put them down the waste chute. Close the windows . . . lock everything . . . The lift wasn't there. Dash down the stairs. Tell the doorman, who managed an impassive reaction while no doubt thinking her plumb crazy.

Then blow the expense and a taxi to the station.

There had been a mid-week football match and the last train was packed. Clare ran along the platform to an accompaniment of catcalls and wolf whistles, and eventually found a space at a table round which four people were meant to sit but which, the five lads already there assured her, could easily take six when one was a little one like her.

On any other day Clare would have felt a wary aloofness, put off by their noisiness and scarves and woolly hats and cans of lager, but tonight she was going back to Monk's Eden to see Adam again. Tonight she loved the whole world.

'Was it a good match?' she asked.

A united groan went up. 'Would have been if we'd won.'

They argued the match from start to finish, with Clare caught mid-way in the stream of banter between two groups of rival supporters. Eventually she suggested moving to the window to allow the argument free rein. There she rested her head against the pane of glass and closed her eyes to the hypnotic rattling of the train along the track, half listening, smiling now and then at some witticism or other.

The voices blurred after a while and she must have dozed a little. Whether it was the stopping of the train at a station that woke her, or the more lively turn the conversation had taken, she didn't know. She only half surfaced, just enough to realise that they had halted and that there was a train at the up platform opposite, then her eyes closed again, her mind only partly absorbing the conversation until their laughter succeeded in fully rousing her.

There seemed to be a shouted exchange going on

with someone on the train opposite. One of them said,

'He's a nutter. He's writing something on the window now.'

'What's it say?' someone else asked. 'Something, then "OFF". And you, mate!' There was another roar of laughter.

Clare's curiosity was coming alive now. She opened her eyes again. The boys were leaning on each other to get near the window and making an assortment of gestures at the train opposite.

She turned to look across the line—and nearly choked with the shock of what she saw.

Someone had written 'GET OFF' with half the letters the wrong way round on a steamed-up patch of the window of the compartment opposite. Someone who was gesturing wildly as she looked, inviting as much wary interest in his own train as in hers. Someone she could hardly believe she was looking at. Adam!

He looked totally different from the icy, controlled stranger she had last spoken to. His dark hair was tousled, his tie yanked loose and the button of his shirt unfastened. And his gestures were getting wilder and wilder until she registered that he was both mouthing and indicating with the sweep of his arm that she should 'GET OFF'.

A whistle blew somewhere, and Clare's mind snapped into action.

'I've got to get off!' she panicked, hemmed in by a forest of jean-clad thighs. She couldn't make sense of Adam being on the London train, but she knew she had to act quickly.

'Got off already, if you ask me!' one of the boys was joking, proud of his word play and enjoying the groan that went up from the others.

'Please!' Another whistle sounded. Something was moving, whether it was their train or the one opposite Clare couldn't tell, but her one-word desperation got through.

'Honest? You really want to go?'

'Yes! I know him. I'm on my way to see him!'

Suddenly legs were squeezing to one side and she was squashing past them. Someone from the end seat at the other side was ahead of her, opening the carriage door. Then she was out, landing on the platform as it seemed to be sliding slowly away from her, stumbling a bit as she made contact, calling a quick 'Thanks' as her bag, which she had completely forgotten, landed with a thud at the side of her. The train picked up rattling speed. More faces joined the boy grinning in the open window. He called out something that Clare didn't quite catch and scarves were waved, but by that time she was not looking.

She was waiting for the last carriage to rock past so that she could look across to the opposite platform and find if Adam had managed it. If not, she had lost her chance of speaking to him tonight, and she was marooned heaven knew where, probably until the first train tomorrow.

At first her heart gave a horrible thud as she thought he wasn't there, but then she saw him jumping down on to the track at the end of the platform and racing across the lines to put a hand on the platform her side and leap up in one impossible bound.

The ticket-collector on duty cried out, 'Here, you can't do that! It's against the regulations.'

But Clare and Adam paid no attention to him. They were clinging to each other, and nothing else mattered.

'You crazy idiot! You didn't look in either direction. You could have been killed!' Clare said, her words clashing with Adam's simultaneous accusation,

'Impossible woman! Why the hell did you go away like that?'

None of the words mattered. She could feel his arms bone-crushingly hard round her, his lean, warm cheek against hers. The world—encapsulated for the moment in the British Rail employee she could hear pounding towards them—could be as hostile as it liked as long as she sensed nothing but love in Adam.

'It's strictly forbidden to cross the line, and you're old enough to know it—sir,' an irate, breathless voice said.

'Oh, I do know it. And I apologise.' Clare, tucked into the hollow of Adam's arm as they turned, found malicious delight in hearing him grovel.

'I couldn't agree more,' she told the man self-righteously. 'I was just saying as much myself.'

'There was nothing else I could do.' Adam prepared to make a good case for himself. 'Imagine—you're on a train and you see the woman you thought you'd never see again in the window of a train going in the opposite direction. You couldn't let her disappear into the distance, could you? Wouldn't you go after her?'

'Can't say that sort of thing happens to me, sir,' the man said stolidly. 'And if it did—yes, I might go after her, but I'd walk over the bridge.' He gave a laconic wave in the appropriate direction. 'Which I hope you will do if you mislay the lady again, sir.'

Clare took the advantage of the softening of his

expression.

'Please—we'll just go into the waiting-room and not worry you any more.'

The man pushed his uniform cap back on his head. 'Well, now, miss, you'd worry me a fair bit if you did that. There's no more trains tonight.'

Adam quietly pressed a note into the man's hand.

'Just a few minutes. We've a lot to say to each other, and if we have to start thinking about how to get anywhere right away, we'll not be able to do it.'

'Talking, is it?' he grinned. 'All right, then. Ten minutes while I finish off, then I'll be wanting to lock up.'

In the waiting-room, Adam would have pulled Clare into his arms again, but she stopped him, determined to have her say, and keeping space between them.

'We've got a lot to talk over, Adam.'

'Damn talking!' His eyes burned into hers, but he thrust his hands impatiently into his pockets and stood waiting.

'You asked why I left. There's a simple answer. I went away because it looked as though that was what you wanted me to do. But it didn't take me long to realise that I wasn't going to give in as easily as all that. I was on my way back now to tell you that you can be as huffy as you like for as long as you like. I intend sticking around in any capacity whatsoever—chauffeur, secretary, anything else you might think of. And if you don't want me as any of those, I'll just find myself a job—but I'll be there whichever way you turn, I warn you, Adam Melvin!'

Her heart was fluttering with fear that she might have overstepped the mark, but Adam was scanning her determined face, her stubbornly lifted chin, with a blend of love and amusement that melted away her nerves.

'Doesn't the fact that I'm here tell you everything, Firecracker?' he said softly.

'I hope so . . . oh, I hope so!' Clare whispered before Adam's kisses took the words from her lips. He kissed her eyes, her temples, the soft skin under her ear, until he finally sighed with deep satisfaction as he rested his face on her hair.

'Oh, Clare! You'll never know the awful feeling of finding you'd gone. And then the frustration of having to chase after you on public transport—not to mention the fact that I only had the vaguest of ideas where you were heading. It's a hell of a thing to happen to someone you love.'

Someone you love . . . Clare cherished the words, stored them away inside her mind to take out and revel in a million times.

'But you came after me.' She leaned back in his arms so that she could see his face and add the way he looked to the wonderful way he sounded. 'What were you going to do?'

'Pound on every door of every flat overlooking the Thames on the Isle of Dogs. That was where Chris said you'd gone.'

She hugged him. 'Why didn't you get Chris to drive you?'

His face expressed sheepish guilt. 'Because he only had one useful eye by then. I closed the other when I lashed out at him for saying that he actually took you to the station.'

'Adam! And he did his level best to stop me, too.'

'I know, I know.' He let go of her and thrust his hands through his dark hair in the way that belonged so uniquely to him. The dark blue eyes looked apologetically into hers. 'It was an instinctive reaction to the awful fear that you might have disappeared for good. Wrong, I know. I'll give him first go at me when we get back. Mrs Kaye will have got the raw steak out.' He reached for her again. 'Clare, I'm a stupid, obstinate fool who acts first and regrets later. Can you forgive me?'

Clare pulled him down on the waiting-room bench beside her.

'If you're willing to listen now, there's nothing to forgive.'

'I'm listening.'

She kept her grip on his arm. After the distance, both physical and emotional, that had been between them, she felt she couldn't be close enough.

'I want to explain about Giles.' She looked into his face, checking that he was listening. 'He wasn't right for me from the start, but at that awful time it just didn't seem to matter. What did matter was that my mother, who knew she was dying, found a kind of calmness that having my future planned gave her. None of us acted normally at that time, Adam. I just drifted into the engagement without really considering what it meant. Then, when I realised afterwards what a ghastly thing I'd done, neither Giles nor my father would listen. They're business partners, and the marriage seemed very appropriate to them. But I knew that I could never make it right if I went through with it. If I hadn't known before I met you, I'd have known it like a bolt from the blue the moment you kissed me. It was . . .' Words failed her, but her eyes made up for her inadequacy.

'I know . . . Like this . . .' Adam's hands cupped her chin, his kiss sent hot magic through her veins. 'For me too,' he said softly.

'You didn't show it. You let me think it was something I was imagining,' Clare said in gentle accusation.

'I'd worked hard on not letting myself make any more mistakes. I fought against everything you did to me—and believe me, you did plenty!'

'And then, just when you'd let yourself begin to trust me, I presented you with what seemed almost a carbon copy of what Fay did. Chris told me a bit more about that to try to make me understand how you felt.'

'Chris can't have told you the whole story, because not even he knows everything,' said Adam. 'You shall know, though, Clare, so that you know why being reminded—however wrongly—of that night affected me as it did.' He reached for her hand and she folded his in both of hers.

'The night Fay left me,' he began, 'I came back a day early from a business trip—missed Fay's car by minutes, Mrs Kaye told me. She didn't know where Fay was going, of course. The note in my study told me that. She was on her way to Harwich so that she could catch the early boat next morning to Denmark. There she would join a man I'd thought a good mutual friend. All tidily over before I got back—only I messed up the timing. The thing that nobody but I—and now you—know, is that Fay had told me a week before I went away that she thought she was pregnant. I knew by that time that the marriage was on the rocks, but if there was a baby involved—my baby—how could I sit back and let her go? It was that knowledge that sent me after her on the Harwich road, driving like a maniac.' He gave a sad little sideways smile at Clare. 'That ghastly night the police saw me and stopped me. While they were questioning me they got an RTA call over their car radio summoning them to an accident further along the A20. I overheard the details while the guy I was talking to was checking my licence and not liking a couple of endorsements I had on it. It was Fay's car that had crashed. I leapt back into mine and drove off to get to her. Somebody had to brake hard when I pulled out, and somebody behind them didn't brake hard enough and went into the back of them. Nothing too dreadful, thank God—I saw that much in my mirror. It all counted against me, naturally enough, when it came to the crunch. I didn't plead mitigating circumstances. I didn't want the fact that Fay was running out on me broadcast. Fay had lost her life . . . that was more than enough. Losing my licence seemed an inadequate punishment for making such a mess of two lives.'

Clare gripped his hand tightly. 'Oh, Adam! And the baby . . .'

'Oh, there was no baby. I learned that at the inquest,' he said levelly. 'That must have been Fay's scheme to make quite sure I kept my distance until she could get away to Denmark.' He looked at Clare. 'Unpleasant facts to stomach. You see why recalling that particular night did so much to me? But not again, Clare. I hit new depths when I thought that my self-indulgent pity had cost me you.' His eyes searched her face. 'I finally put Fay where she should have been for months—in the past. I'll never deny that I found her physically attractive—that was always strong. But I fooled myself when I married her that it was enough to base a marriage on . . . and it wasn't. It *isn't*. It has to be there, but there's so much more . . .' His fingers traced a loving path over Clare's features. 'And if you're inclined to deduce from that that physical attraction is in second place with you, my love, I'm prepared to spend the rest of my life showing you just how wrong an assumption that is. Your Giles . . . my Fay . . . without them we couldn't have compared what we had then with what we have now. For that we must thank them.'

Clare brought his hand to her lips and kissed it. 'And now that there's no more mystery, we understand each other so perfectly.'

He kissed her again, a long, satisfying kiss which, paradoxically, left them both hungry for more.

'The only remaining mystery,' Adam said eventually, 'is exactly where we are.'

'There must be a station sign somewhere.'

They stood and peered out into the deserted station.

'Witham,' said Adam. 'A bit of an unknown quantity as far as I'm concerned. Maybe we'll know a whole lot more about it by morning. What are you smiling at?'

'I've just realised what that boy shouted at me from the train. "Enjoy yourself Witham"!'

Adam groaned. 'What boy?'

She gave him an impish grin. 'Just another person with whom I struck up a quick relationship.'

'Don't make a habit of it.' He pulled her close and continued instructing her in habits he fully approved of.

'Finished talking yet?' the ticket collector enquired with malicious enjoyment of what he was interrupting.

They broke apart, but Adam was completely unruffled.

'I've a feeling that conversations of that kind will go on for a very long time indeed,' he said with a wicked grin.

They followed the British Rail man to the exit.

'And while all these conversations are going on,' said Clare as they went towards the phone booth the man had indicated, 'shall I be acting as secretary, chauffeur, or what?' She thought—*believed*—that she knew the answer, but it hadn't been said in so many words.

Adam pretended to study the question.

'I already have a perfectly good secretary, as you pointed out. And the driving ban expires next week, so I shan't need a chauffeur. There's nothing else for it. I've got a brand new wedding ring that's come all the way from Italy with nobody to wear it. And after all, we did waste an awful lot of opportunity in Sicily, didn't we? So I think, all in all, you'd better take on the job of wife, if you can bear it.'

Clare's heart lifted and beat a rejoicing tattoo, but she kept up his deadpan attitude.

'I can bear it. And if you're behind a wheel again, a backseat driver wouldn't come amiss, I imagine.'

Adam burst out laughing and pulled her into the phone booth with him, putting the confined space to a use for which it had never been intended.

Clare suddenly remembered his trip to London that morning.

'Adam, your film! What happened at the meeting?'

'They're going to wait.' His arms tightened round her, his lips close to hers as he said, 'Didn't I tell you I always get what I want?'

GIFT OF GOLD *Jayne Ann Krentz* **£3.50**

One dark night in Mexico, Verity Ames tantalized a knight in shining armour – Jonas Quarrel. To release himself from a tormenting nightmare, he was compelled to track her down and discover all her secrets…

A WILD WIND *Evelyn A. Crowe* **£2.99**

Ten years ago, Shannon Reed and Ash Bartlet had planned to marry, but disaster struck. Now they have been given a second chance, until Shannon is accused of murder…

SHARE MY TOMORROW *Connie Bennett* **£2.75**

It was a dream come true for marine biologist, Lillian Lockwood – not only working with the renowned submarine pilot, Neal Grant, but finding such happiness together. But only by confronting his ghosts could Neal bury the memories which were crippling their love.

These three new titles will be out in bookshops from April 1990

WORLDWIDE

Available from Boots, Martins, John Menzies, W.H. Smith, Woolworths and other paperback stockists.

Questionnaire

A Free Mills & Boon Romance for you!

At Mills & Boon we always do our best to ensure that our books are just what you want to read. To do this we need your help! Please spare a few minutes to answer the questions below and overleaf and, as a special thank you, we will send you a FREE Mills & Boon Romance when you return your completed questionnaire.

Don't forget to fill in your name and address so we know where to send your FREE BOOK.

Please tick the appropriate boxes to indicate your answers.

1 (a) **Are you a regular Mills & Boon Romance reader?**

Yes ❑ No ❑

(b) **If you are, how many Romances do you read each month?**

1 ❑ 2-4 ❑ 4-6 ❑ more than 6 ❑

2 **We'd like your views on which season your Romances are set in:-**

(a) **For example would you mind reading a book set at Christmas in July?**

Yes ❑ No ❑ Don't mind ❑

(b) **Would you prefer to read about hot summery settings in the Summer and winter settings in the Winter?**

Yes ❑ No ❑ Don't mind ❑

3 (a) **Would you like to read about older heroines?**

Yes ❑ No ❑ Don't mind ❑

Please complete overleaf

(b) **If yes, from which age group, please tick one to indicate your choice.**

in their thirties? ❑ forties? ❑ fifties? ❑

4 Do you like the hero to be older than the heroine?

Yes ❑ No ❑ Don't mind ❑

5 In your view what is the ideal age gap between hero and heroine?

5 years ❑ 10 years ❑ 20 years ❑ No age gap ❑

6 Is there anything you particularly like or dislike about Mills & Boon books?

____

____

7 What is your favourite type of book apart from romantic fiction?

____

____

8 What age group are you in?

Under 25 ❑ 25-34 ❑
35-54 ❑ 55-65 ❑
Over 65 please state______

9 Are you a Reader Service subscriber?

Yes ❑ No ❑

Thank you for your help. We hope that you enjoy your FREE book.

Post this page TODAY TO: Mills & Boon Reader Survey FREEPOST, P.O. Box 236, Croydon CR9 9EL.

EDQ3

Mr/Mrs/Ms/Miss ______________________________

Address ______________________________

____

____

______________________________ Postcode ______________